Without a Party

Without a Party

A Story of Romance and
Politics in a Nation Divided

Terri Mudd

MOUNTAIN ARBOR
PRESS

MOUNTAIN ARBOR
PRESS
Alpharetta, GA

ISBN: 978-1-63183-014-3

Library of Congress Control Number: 2016955743

10 9 8 7 6 5 4 3 2   1 1 0 3 1 6

Printed in the United States of America

♾This paper meets the requirements of ANSI/NISO Z39.48-1992 (Permanence of Paper)

Cover art and illustrations by DeSales Kellick

This work is dedicated to President Jimmy Carter, another president who endured poor treatment by the press and the public yet valiantly mastered the art of survival in a trying political atmosphere. It is both uplifting and exemplary that Mr. Carter went on to prevail in tireless humanitarian work after leaving the presidency and earn his well-deserved place in the history of our nation.

Contents

Acknowledgments

In many ways this was a family project. All three of my sons, Mike, Kevin, and Andy, made major contributions in the areas of advice, finance, and equipment. My daughters, Margaret and Mary, contributed no less in their general patience with a possessed parent, critiquing, proofreading, and in the case of Ellen, helping to keep my nose to the grindstone and living with me as I put the book together. All along, Kevin encouraged my every effort and Andy set a fine example by his faith in the written word. My five grandchildren gave me day-to-day reason to keep going and never give up; and my husband, Jim, who was with me in life and in death.

My editor, Bob Giannetti, suffered with my oddities, inconsistencies, poor work habits, and terrible punctuation.

DeSales Kellick, my lifelong friend and artist extraordinaire, created portraits of the principle characters of the novel and gave visual realization to a crucial event in the story which became the cover art for the book.

Jeanne Crump helped to resolve persistent human and computer errors, enabling me to produce a readable manuscript.

I owe an untold debt of gratitude to Robert Seager II, author of the definitive biography of President Tyler, *And

Tyler Too (New York: McGraw Hill, 1963). His meticulous research turned up many juicy details that made their way into my piece of historical fiction. In deference to Mr. Seager, I have provided notes that document my use of direct quotations of original, historical source materials he included in his biography.

And also my thanks to Irving Stone, whose wonderful biographical novels gave me a lifetime of reading pleasure while learning how to go about writing such a novel. I've tried to follow in his footsteps by telling a true story in a fictional form, thus lending life to historical characters that jump out of their biographies.

CHRONICLE NEWS

ALL THE NEWS
ALL THE TIME

February 28, 1844

Washington, DC, 3:00 p.m.

A fatal explosion occurred aboard the USS *Princeton*, a new steam frigate, while it was traveling down river on the Potomac. On board were John Tyler, president of the United States, and most of his close advisors and friends. He was entertaining the city's elite. Some of that chosen number did not make it back to shore alive.

On board were men who forged the destiny of the country: Secretary of State Abel Upshur; Thomas

Gilmer, secretary of navy; Virgil Maxey, former chief of delegation at The Hague; and David Gardiner, personal friend and advisor to the president. All these gentlemen perished in the unexplained explosion of a cannon mounted on the deck called "the Peacemaker." Among the wounded are Thomas Hart Benton and nine seamen. The president's personal valet was also killed in the incident.

The cannon was successfully discharged several times before the fatal accident. As the ship passed Washington's estate, the crowd called for one more shot to honor the first president. Tyler, who was below deck, paused momentarily before going to the scene to hear his son-in-law, William Waller, finish the song: "Eight hundred men lay slain . . ." Without that delay, the country might well have discovered what happens when neither a president nor a vice president is available to serve the country. Tyler succeeded to the presidency after Harrison's death. A new vice president was not named.

The SS *Johnston*, a ship nearby, carried the able-bodied back to shore. The president himself was seen carrying the limp body of Julia Gardiner, a debutante whose name has been socially associated with his. Miss Gardiner's father, a state senator from New York and advisor to the president, was among the fatalities.

Chapter 1

New York City, 1836
Julia's Coming-Out Party

Julia, aged seventeen, moved in front of the mirror, alternating between hugging herself and sailing into an imaginary breeze in a torrent of motion.

"Land sakes, girl, quit wrigglin' until I get the dress square on you." Eliza Brumley was attempting to pull the dress over Julia's head, lay the plaits in place, and square the silver buckle, all at the same time.

"I can't. I'm too excited. Today is the most important day of my life."

"Most important so far," Eliza Brumley, her aunt, corrected.

Young Julia Gardiner, swathed in fine white lace, the silver buckle exactly where it showed her tiny waist to the best advantage, turned her gaze from the mirror to her aunt.

"You're right, I know. There will be other days like this one. Still, I can hardly wait! Until tonight I was a child. Now, I'm a . . ." She stopped, returned her gaze to the reflection, and smoothed her deep, rich brown curls over her ears, "woman." She heard the eerie change in her own voice. It was a woman's resonant contralto, not a teenaged cry.

Eliza, cousin and close friend of the family, had been chosen to prepare Julia for her coming-out ball at Mrs. Chagaray's Finishing School for Young Ladies. She pinned the nosegay at the base of Julia's neckline, suggesting—just suggesting—a décolletage. Julia stood motionless, willing herself to be a statue for her aunt. When Eliza stepped back to admire the handiwork, Julia turned again to the mirror, raised her arms with a dance-like motion, and faintly curtsied to the reflection. The older woman beamed with satisfaction.

"It's too bad your mama can't see you tonight." Eliza moved a curl carefully to fall beside Julia's cheek.

Julia was matter-of-fact. "Papa said they really were obligated to attend the gala in Albany. I don't see why Mr. Van Buren had to choose tonight for his party." Although she was disappointed, as she looked in the mirror again, she smiled. "But that's the way it is when you're important. Duty calls. Someday it will be me, and duty will demand I look this way every night. I will have to be in important places, doing wonderful things." Gaslight cast a shadow in the room, muting the colors and contrasting sharply with Julia's mood. It lent soft tones and a dreamlike quality to her irrepressible love of life that might otherwise have appeared frenetic.

Eliza folded the last pleat and patted her shoulder. "You're just right, not overstated. Julia, you understand, don't you, that there will be more elaborate gowns there tonight?"

"But none will be this perfect. I feel like a fairy princess. Tonight shall be perfection. I just know it."

"You make your own magic, Julia. You'll never have to worry." Eliza finished her task with great care, dimmed the light, and held the door as Julia pirouetted out, moving to the parlor where Rueben, Eliza's husband, and Alexander, Julia's elder brother, waited.

As they approached the two men, Alex's expression made clear the preparations were a success. "The little goose has turned into a swan," he said over her head to Eliza.

Julia's large brown eyes danced. "Do you really like it?"

Her older brother bowed deeply. "I shall be the envy of every cadet and," he turned to his uncle, "every other man in the room this evening. Shall we go?" Rueben's vigorous nod affirmed his judgment.

Alex placed Julia's cape on her shoulders as they moved into the rainy April evening where the carriage was waiting. He extended his arm to Julia as they headed for the staircase. The foursome was on its way to Mrs. Chagaray's School for Young Ladies.

Inside the carriage, the rain could be heard on the roof. Horses' hooves clopped along the street, echoing. The foursome rode in silence until Julia, bubbling over, could no longer endure the quiet.

"I do wish Mama and Papa were with us." In the dark, she could only sense Alex's smile.

He said, "They had to be in Albany tonight. Mr. Van Buren may be our next president, you know."

"But I'm here, and this is the most important minute in my life!"

Alex laughed out loud. He reached out to touch his little sister's face. "There will be many more, Julia. Mother and Father have great confidence that you are just beginning."

Eliza added, "Indeed, I wonder if your mother knows how important this event is to you. I'm surprised Juliana is missing it."

Alex turned to Eliza. "She knows, but she also knows that Julia has tremendous resources of her own."

Rueben asked, "Is Senator Gardiner supporting Van Buren?"

Alex hesitated, then answered, "I don't think Father has any great love for him. This Jackson business is out of hand. He seems to feel Van Buren will be the new occupant of the White House. Van is supposed to be Jackson's man, but he isn't Jackson. And the others don't know what they're doing. Whigs are running Hugh White in the South, Webster in Massachusetts, and Harrison on the frontier, each with a different running mate."

As the cab pulled up in front of the hotel, Rueben and Alex turned their attention to getting the ladies out of the cab and into the building without allowing the rain to affect them.

The reception hall glittered with candlelight reflecting from the chandeliers. Julia marveled at the crystal and candles that gave a warm glow to the room and the crowd. Everyone was here tonight. At first she saw only one or two of her classmates, their parents, and the teaching staff.

The rest of the gathering seemed to be composed of the elite of New York City. In the background, strains of music could be heard.

The headmistress, Mrs. Chagaray, the Latin teacher, Mr. Quinn, and Miss Mallac, the music teacher, formed the reception line. Julia, on Alex's arm and followed by Eliza and Rueben, made her way to the director of the school. As they approached the line, Julia sensed a change. She felt as if she were on display in some undefined manner.

"What's happening, Alex?" she whispered.

"They're spellbound by the look of the lovely maiden on my arm, as every person in the room will be before the night is over." He finished just in time to greet Mrs. Chagaray. Julia presented her brother and the Brumleys. They passed through the line and into a small collection of students and parents, where Julia made appropriate introductions.

She and her good friend Ernestine Hiller admired each other's dresses. Ernestine was shorter than Julia. She had flaxen blond hair and blue eyes that always seemed to laugh. Mr. Hiller, Ernestine's father, showed the same patrician heritage, minus the laughter. He engaged Alex in conversation in a manner that suggested little patience with the social affair in which he found himself. "Gardiner, are you the senator's son?"

"My father is a member of the New York State Senate, yes. I'm impressed that you are that aware of Long Island politics." Alex had one eye on the evening's events, even as they chatted. He was in charge of his sister's well-being.

"Ah, yes, he's a good man. Can't be too careful these days, what with hotheads everywhere." Mr. Hiller was intent upon engaging Alex as if they were at the club.

"Dad's conservative enough," said Alex, as his eyes followed Julia. He gave only scant attention to Mr. Hiller's pontification.

"What's he think about this Texas uprising? Houston's out of line. He's going to get us into a shootin' match with Mexico! We should just stop all this nonsense now. We've enough land to digest. I'm not sure Jefferson should have annexed the Ohio Valley. Look at the trouble the frontier is giving!"

Alex caught Julia's eye. "Mr. Hiller, it's been good talking to you. I'm sure we'll see more of each other over the evening." He turned and took Julia's arm for the promenade.

Head held high, she moved in unison with her big brother. The handsome couple followed the line, awaiting greetings. Julia was not tall, but her regal bearing, the graceful white gown, and the cap of dark curls created a vision that allowed her to dominate the Grand March. Led by Mrs. Chagaray and Mr. Quinn, the girls, their escorts, and their parents were followed by the other guests in the promenade. When the music stopped, the ranks broke again into sociable groups. Then a waltz began.

Julia's first dance was with Alex. Then as the next number opened, Mr. Hiller, who had placed his name on her dance card, intercepted. As the music started, he approached Julia, took her arm, and moved toward the dance floor. She glanced at Alex, who placed his fingers on his forehead in a salute that said, "You are on your own, little sister!"

"Are you really so opposed to expansion?" Julia asked the gentleman, as if she had been part of the earlier conversation.

Confusion was written over his face, and then, enlightenment. "Ah, you were eavesdropping?"

"No, listening. Such matters are important. They are frequently discussed at our house."

Mr. Hiller hesitated for just a moment, then he laughed aloud. "You are a most unusual young lady!"

Their eyes met.

She bowed her head slightly, as if to agree.

After the dance, Alex rescued her from Hiller's company. However, he placed her into the hands of the nearest cadet who was also seeking her attention. Robert Cividon, a tall, blond young man in a nearby military-academy uniform, lined up with her. Julia had sufficient sense of rhythm to save them from collision or from looking as awkward as they might.

"You dance well," he offered with a shy grin.

"I think dancing is more of a women's art. Men just tag along." Julia gave him her most endearing smile.

"Well, it's not something we learn at military school."

She laughed gently. "Did you learn to get punch for a thirsty dance partner?"

Once off the dance floor, Robert regained some poise. They sipped punch and discussed the incessant rain pouring outdoors. Julia guided the conversation. "What do you study in military school?"

"Science, philosophy, military history, rhetoric. What do girls study?"

"Nothing that interesting, believe me."

Alex again liberated her. He was chuckling as they started to waltz. "Who was leading? I hope you allowed him some shred of dignity. I have the definite sense that you two were not an equal match."

"He was a child."

"This world is composed of children and old men, dear. You must walk between them and take your pick."

"I shall have neither. I want a prince who will care for me like Papa does and adore me like . . ."

"Like I do?"

"No, better than that—he won't tease me. He won't call me a goose."

"Maybe by the time that you find him, you won't be a goose. Tonight I have hope that you will eventually reign supreme!"

The rest of evening was a blur of girls' fathers, cadets, and Alex orchestrating Julia's attentions. Through it all, Julia did not lose her sense of being in control. This was her life, her party, her world.

Later that night she was far too excited to sleep. She lay for a long time, just thinking, remembering, feeling the evening again.

"*. . . That you will reign supreme . . .*" *All of life will be like tonight. I want romance, knowledge, money, power, love. I want* *it all. I wonder how women survive. They run around with eyes cast down, only nodding. They never say anything. They've never asked the important questions. I don't think I could live a life confined to plays and whist and the stain on the imported sofa! I'll have to ask Mama.*

Thus, Julia drifted off on the first day of her adult life.

Chapter 2

John Is a Politician of Principle

John Tyler rose from behind his desk to conclude the interview. Two of his three guests prepared to leave. Henry Wise also stood up, but he turned his back on the farewells and moved to the window, now framing a view of the rainy day outside.

Senator Calhoun, the huge, white-haired gentleman from South Carolina, spoke: "If you make it a point of personal honor, we have nothing more to say."

Tyler, the tallest man, said, "Thank you for your concern. The first act of my political life was to censure my colleagues, because they refused to follow the instructions of the Virginia Assembly, to whom they were pledged, and with whom they did not agree. The Virginia House of Delegates in 1811 instructed them to vote against the renewal of the National Bank. They did not comply, and I was responsible for the censure action taken against them."

He put out his hand to the giant from South Carolina and turned to the red-haired senator from Kentucky.

"Senator Clay, I appreciate your interest in my continued service. But my conscience makes demands of me that expediency cannot override."

Clay nodded. "Of course, sir. We understand, but inasmuch as our common goal is to rid ourselves of that tyrant Jackson in the White House, we hoped you would consider staying, casting your vote, and accepting censure."

Tyler nodded. "I trust you understand that my conscience dictates this course of action."

When Clay and Calhoun departed, Tyler faced Henry Wise, his friend and confidante. "What was that all about, really, Henry?"

Henry blinked his pale blue eyes, while behind him the rain splashed on the window pane as the scene darkened into evening. "You heard. They want you to remain in the Senate."

"Why? They've never wanted me any place but on my farm before now."

Wise moved from the window to Tyler's desk. Somewhat shorter than John, he seemed to stretch to make their eyes meet. "Really, John, I think you are overstating the case. They respect your intellect and integrity."

"Henry Clay would not recognize integrity if it were the plague!" Tyler snapped, and then seemed to relax. He returned to his chair. "I think my presence would be of some material benefit to them, and I want to know what is."

Wise, although younger, was the senior warrior. "Would it make a difference if you did know?"

"No, of course not! The right of the States to instruct a United States senator is an absolute. You know that. I must resign."

"I'm much less certain of absolutes than you, John. That's why I admire you so greatly." Wise returned to the window, giving John the opportunity to reflect.

After a lengthy silence, Tyler said, "This time, my certainties have gotten me into a real dilemma. On one hand, if I vote as I believe, I'm ignoring the instruction of the body to which I'm responsible. If I follow the dictates of Virginia, I'd be voting against the very foundation of the Union, and that merely to obtain a narrow goal. Clearly resignation is my only answer."

"You've never really been happy in politics, have you?"

"Politics is in my blood. At least I thought it was. But Andy Jackson has changed what I thought I knew to be politics."

"In '32 you supported him."

"Adams was the issue then. Besides, it was different; Jackson stood well on the bank issue, or so I thought. It turned out, his solution to the problem was worse than the bank itself. Then, there's patronage. He has chopped through any decent form of government as if the whole forest were his. And he has usurped power proper to the Legislature."

Tyler rubbed his graying temples and returned to Wise's question. "Politics has turned sour since that man entered the scene. I remember sitting at the dinner table with my father and President Jefferson. The talk was about integrity then, how to govern with wisdom and enter into relationships with other states—with justice. Fairness and justice are issues that don't seem to be important anymore. Jackson has ruined national politics. He's taken something honorable and good and prostituted it. Now, politics is power, raw and ugly. It will tear the country apart—eventually, there will be no fixing the situation!"

Wise measured his words. "You know, even Jefferson had to consider power and support. Politics has always been with us."

"Andrew Jackson sullied politics. He's made it crude and filthy. And it hasn't come out of the mire. Clay stoops as low as Jackson."

"John, he has to compromise—there's no other way. It's like a magic box; once opened . . ." His voice trailed off.

John looked steadily at Wise. "Nothing goes back into the box, does it?"

Henry turned to the window in time to see two familiar figures moving along under the street lamp. The taller man held an umbrella that protected both of them from the rain.

***

Calhoun and Clay made their way down the street toward the hotel. Clay muttered, "Righteous pig!"

"Easy, Senator. When his conscience is on our side, we appreciate him. He stands with me on the right of the State to nullify national legislation. He's good on power issues."

"How can we ever appreciate him, sir? He's stiff-necked, supercilious, arrogant!" Clay spit out the words.

Calhoun chuckled. "I think the real reason for your ire is that he is an embarrassment to the Whig party that you love so dearly."

"He's an embarrassment to the human race. Prig!"

"The day may come when you need him, righteousness and all."

"I hope to God, not so!"

***

Wise, at the window, followed the black umbrella and the two men it sheltered until they went out of sight. He moved from the window to the seat across from John. He brought the subject back to the immediate question. "You don't mistrust Calhoun the way you do Clay."

"Calhoun is different. He may wreak havoc in the nation with his nullification scheme, but it won't be from rot. The difference is that he's a man of principle. I trust him, but I don't always agree with him." Tyler pushed his hair back, as if trying to rid himself of unpleasant realities.

Silence weighed on the room. The gaslight flickered.

"You know, John Tyler, of the absolutes. Clay, as much as you despise him, points the way you will have to go someday. Calhoun will save our beloved South, but he will destroy the Union. Webster will abolish slavery at all costs, and cry when the South secedes. Clay will hold us together, and the South will have integrity, but he will do it by compromise."

John stared out the window. Horses splashed in the mud as carriages rode by. The rain tapped steadily on the window. "That's an interesting point. Clay's ability to negotiate everything is troublesome to me. Yet, I know the zealots are wrong."

"Is there a difference between an absolutist and a zealot?" Henry asked. "I've never considered you a zealot, but you do speak of absolutes. That's why you are about to return home now."

Tyler's face softened. His eyes and mouth began to suggest a grin in the making. He seemed boyish, disarming. "You make it sound as if I'm an absolutist and Clay is a zealot, and that's the only difference. You give much to think about, my friend, as I go forth into the winter of my own discontent."

The next day, February 29, 1836, Tyler submitted his letter of resignation to the House of Delegates in Virginia. It was accepted. John did not feel particularly missed. He knew that he was both loved and hated in the Senate. There seemed to be few men of his persuasion anywhere these days. Plans to replace him were already abounding in the Whig caucus in Washington City and at home in Virginia. But temporarily, at least, politics were removed from center stage in John's life.

***

John could feel his pulse increase as he neared home. The carriage ride from Washington had been torturous. A day on horseback from Richmond to Williamsburg was worse. He knew he would receive a warm greeting from Letitia, but he did not know what to expect from Tazewell. Taz had been a baby when he left to go to Washington. Trips home had been short and less frequent than he wanted. John knew his absence had taken its toll on a relationship with his youngest.

Taz's birth had been difficult for Letitia. Twenty-five years of childbearing was not easy for a woman. Circumstances exacerbated the situation. The older children were adults, and their problems were greater. John feared Letitia was physically weakened, lacking stamina, and emotionally drained from the stress of parenting without his help. *Well, at least now I can be with them. Maybe, with my company and the easing of her responsibility, I can bring Letitia around to her old self.*

John saw her, tall and frail, waiting at the door. She wore grey gingham with an elegance that made it seem one of the finest of materials. Her radiant smile filled him with tenderness.

The manservant took his horse, and John hurried to her. As he folded her into his arms, she seemed even more fragile than he remembered.

"I'm so glad you are here, my dear." Her words were few and simple, directly from her heart. He said nothing. The quiet between them spoke of a deeply desired reunion. He could feel her shoulders. Her slender hands, as they touched his face to trace lines, were like a balm.

"Home—this time it's for good."

Letitia distanced herself from his embrace and looked up into his eyes. "Don't promise too much, my love."

***

Later, John mounted his horse and called Taz. "Come on, boy. Let's go over to the fields and see what's happening."

Taz jumped from the tree he was climbing and hurried to his father's side. John lifted him onto the saddle and climbed up behind him. They trotted off at a leisurely pace.

"Are you goin' to stay home now, Papa?" Taz twisted just slightly. John could see his profile, so much like Letitia's.

"I think so, son. Farming is good for the soul. I can't say the same for politics."

"Why not?"

John realized that he was talking over the boy's head, trying to clear his own thoughts. He squeezed Taz affectionately. "Not to worry, boy. You and I will stick to our farm for now. When you get older we'll talk about politics."

They came to the clearing. When the field workers recognized him, they straightened up from their work to respond to his greeting. "Howdy, Massa Tyler."

He dismounted, swung down, and allowed Taz to hold the reins.

"Hello, boys. The work is coming well."

The men returned to work except the crew leader. He came over to discuss plans for clearing and sowing. "De plot over there tomorrow, and we'll do 'de east side next week. By then, time to plant will be comin' on."

"Josh, you do a fine job of planning work. Will nature help us out with rain at the right time and sun when we need it?"

Josh beamed at the praise. "It's due to be a good year, Massa John. I think we do jes' fine!"

"How's the soil? Here, let me see." He took Josh's hoe and slid in beside his men working the earth. The black men noted their master at work. "It feels just right. Maybe tomorrow I'll join you in the early part of the day to see how it goes."

"That be right good, Massa." John felt a kinship with the responsible foreman. He knew what it was to walk a fine line between driving his workers and encouraging them. He also knew that many plantation owners never did the work they asked others to do.

He returned to Taz and mounted the horse. They rode down by the James River and around through town. It was late afternoon when they returned home. John was hungry and tired. He knew that he would eat a good evening meal and sleep the night through, luxuries he did not enjoy in Washington.

When the last of the daylight disappeared, John and Letitia sat together. Letitia's fingers moved, pulling the needle in and out as she replaced buttons, repaired small tears, and let down the hems in Taz's pants. "That boy is growing. I think he will be taller than you, dear. He's all leg."

John set down the paper. "He certainly seems to enjoy life. Has he been as easygoing all year as he seems?"

"Oh, Taz is fine," Letitia responded deliberately. She concentrated on her handwork.

"But?" John heard the question in her statement

"It's been a difficult year, John. The harvest was just mediocre. The men in the field worked well, but they can't place wealth where there is none."

"Nor can I, my dear. But we will work the soil, and I can establish a practice in law again. Between the two, we will survive."

"We always have." She did not raise her eyes.

"I'm so glad to be home. Washington life is terrible. My stomach cannot abide boarding house food. I need your tender care and attention."

"And we need you." Letitia took a button from her sewing basket, threaded a needle, and repaired Tazewell's shirt.

Chapter 3

Williamsburg, 1837
A Dubious Commendation for John

The letter from the Virginia caucus of Whigs surprised Tyler. It was an invitation to come to Richmond for a dinner at which he and Senator Benjamin Leigh, who had continued to serve in the Senate, were both to be honored. Leigh had ignored the instructions of the Virginia Assembly, while John, honoring the right of that body to instruct him, had resigned rather than defy them. Obviously, John decided, there must be some mistake. Both men could not be right. John set the invitation aside, dismissing it, until a delegation of Virginia Whigs including Henry Wise visited him.

It was not Wise who led the group, but a pompous gentleman unknown to Tyler who held out his ham-like paw and introduced himself. "Senator Hugh Downey here, sir." He then presented the other stranger to Tyler. "And this is John Whitcomb."

Tyler acknowledged both newcomers and Wise, to whom John gave a quizzical look.

Downey came to the point at once. "We've come to request your presence at a dinner honoring you and Senator Leigh.

We appreciate your valiant choice to resign rather than violate your conscience; an admirable stance, indeed!"

John's reaction was guarded. He wanted to speak to his trusted friend, Wise, in private, but circumstances did not allow it. John said, "But gentlemen, Senator Leigh did not resign—he just ignored the instruction. How can you deal with us together? We did not see either the problem or the solution in the same light. It hardly seems appropriate to unite recognition of such diverse solutions."

Downey cleared his throat and folded his hands. Tyler was reminded of a preacher about to grant forgiveness. "Well, you see, sir, who is right is not the issue. You both voted your conscience, and that is the important mark of a statesman. You chose different means of expression, but your integrity is equally admirable. And that is what we choose to honor."

The dubious logic of the commendation he was about to receive troubled Tyler, but, encouraged by Letitia, he appeared at the dinner and received his award graciously, never losing the feeling that he was being manipulated.

After the dinner he and Henry were going to their rooms at the hotel in Richmond. Wise was silent; Tyler, thoughtful.

Suddenly the award made sense: Wise had a plan. "Henry, you are responsible for this circus, aren't you?"

Wise looked at the floor, not meeting Tyler's eyes. They walked along the hallway to Henry's door. "Come on in for a nightcap." Henry opened the door. John followed him into the room. The gaslight cast shadows. Wise turned it up to brighten the room. A Spartan bed with two chairs and a small table filled the room. A decanter of whiskey rested on the table. "What now, John?" Wise poured the amber liquid into snifters and each man settled in a chair.

Tyler sat tall; the chair complemented his long, slender body. "We seem to be going for the lowest common denominator: opposition to Jackson and his ally, Van Buren."

Shorter than John, Wise looked vaguely ridiculous in the chair opposite. His feet did not comfortably touch the floor. "By not having a platform, we don't have to deal with industrialization, trade, tariff or agrarian issues. Nothing separates the party into factions. We can keep New York and western Whigs together with ourselves. By making only minimal promises, ones we can keep, we hold the South, New York Whigs, and the frontier. That means we keep both Daniel Webster and Calhoun. We need them all—and you too, my friend." Wise, full of nervous energy, left his seat and paced around the room.

Tyler said, "But to keep all of us . . . well, you just can't do that, Henry. As soon as the election is over, we will have to face those issues, and we have nothing in common."

"Oh yes, we have; we all want the Union to remain just that—a Union!" Wise proclaimed as he paced the room, "Compromise. John—you may not like it, but if we are going to remain one nation we must never lose sight of that goal. We must defeat Van Buren and begin to repair Jackson's damage, or Cal will push the right of a state to nullify a federal action on some damned issue, and we'll have secession and war."

"It's not just Cal that's difficult, you know." Now Tyler turned to face Henry. "Dan Webster is like the marble from New Hampshire where he was born. And Clay is deceitful, manipulative."

Wise smiled, easing the tension, as he settled again in his chair. "No one can accuse you of being deceitful or manipulative. But you, too, my friend, can be difficult. With Francis Pickens, we can keep Calhoun in check. We can carry South Carolina. And Clay can manage the frontier vote. God knows we can't afford to lose a marginal state if we are going to beat Van Buren. And Webster—well, he knows the stakes are high."

Tyler studied his drink in silence. He turned to another problem. "These conventions, they throw too much responsibility on the individual. I don't like their looks. The Democrats had one this year. The Whigs are caucusing in some places with elected officials. Conventions obtain in other states. It seems to me conventions deny the primacy of the state."

Wise poured himself another draught of whiskey and settled in for the kill. "Indeed, four years ago we saw the first national convention ever. The system is going to come, John, mark my words. Maybe not in '36 nor '40, but before many more elections go by. The convention is an idea that the people are ready for."

"That takes responsibility from the very men popularly elected to exercise it. We don't know what we are doing. What happens to our sovereignty? The system will lead to mob rule. I don't trust conventions. A caucus in the lower house of each state will do just fine." Tyler appeared to be studying the remains of his drink, not watching his cherubic host.

"John, keep up with the times. Since Jackson got it into his head that the Democrats should nominate by convention, it has gained popularity. If we are going to beat them, we must use their way. The people want it."

"But, Henry, we formed a government of states. The popular voice at home elects the state legislature."

"Don't be too sure that system will last. Out in Ohio and in Kentucky you see populists' will reflected all the time. That's how they are doing things in the young part of the country. We must capitalize on that kind of thinking."

"But when the elected officials get around to governing, will they remember that it was the states that elected them? What happens to state sovereignty in this populist upheaval?"

"What do you mean?" Henry emptied the snifter.

"I don't know how deep this populist thing runs when you consider the country as a whole. You use Ohio and Kentucky as examples. But in the East, business controls the newspapers, and newspapers control the populist electorate. So who's doing the electing?"

"It's not that bad, John."

"The so-called populists have lost sight of what or who is the sovereign. Calhoun may go too far, but he is ultimately right. We are a nation of states." John took the last sip.

"John, face facts. The Whig Party, if you can call it that, is a mongrel. Some Whigs are Federalists and some are states' rights people. Most of them don't really know what they are. All we really have in common is the need to beat Van Buren. Clay's willing to take a chance on a convention. So is Webster."

Tyler added, "Yes, Clay—whichever way the wind blows, he'll have his kite up just to make sure the power ends in his hands."

"He is supporting the convention idea. So is Webster, and he is the ultimate aristocrat."

"If Clay is supporting it then he thinks he can win that way. He can't afford to go against Webster and the easterners. He wants to be president so badly that he'd sell his soul—if he hasn't already."

Tyler set his glass down. As Wise tried to refill it, he covered it and shook his head. "No more. My stomach was ruined in Washington City."

Henry pursued his argument, "Well, we watched the Democrats name Van Buren and Johnson in convention last winter. The Whigs had better offer a popular candidate or Van Buren will win."

"Well, I will be watching from behind a plow. It's home and family for me from now on." Tyler prepared to leave.

Henry rose as he did and said, "Don't close us out, John. There are too few men like yourself, men of principle, in office today."

As they reached the door, Tyler opened it and turned to his friend. "Doesn't seem to hold much promise for integrity these days, Henry. Good night."

Chapter 4

1839

Julia Is Introduced to Financial Realities

"But Papa, we always go to Newport or Saratoga or somewhere!" Julia was near tears.

"Well, this year we will spend a month at Gardiner's Island. You may reacquaint yourself with your cousins."

Juliana, Julia's mother, said, "Julia, go to your room. Your father and I will discuss this."

David interposed, "I believe Julia should hear this."

Juliana was surprised at her husband's intervention but did not contradict him.

David's manner changed subtly. "The land is in an economic state known as 'depression.' Do you ladies understand what that means?"

Juliana was taken aback by her husband's reproach. "Yes, of course. We read about it in the paper all the time."

"Papa, does that mean we don't have enough money?" Julia sounded concerned.

"No, Julia, for us the problem is not that immediate. But it does mean that for now, we are dependent on current rents from our properties in the city for income. And our savings for the future . . . not only are they not increasing, but they may be shrinking."

Julia's face registered both concern and a desire to learn more. "But others?"

"People who live very near the edge, day workers and small businessmen, are hurting. And laborers, immigrants, and farmers are suffering seriously."

Juliana intervened. "But must we punish our family?"

"My dear, you make a wonderful mother and an altogether superior partner. But you do not seem to understand that depression and panic, closed banks, and defaulting businesses do affect our personal life."

"I've always managed my personal funds to good advantage." Juliana straightened her back and confronted David.

"You've always managed to spend them." David said as he patted her shoulder. "That's not quite the same as managing to keep them in existence when banks are withholding specie and worse—failing."

"Do you mean . . .?" Juliana's voice trailed off as she began to absorb the nature and extent of the crisis.

"Yes, I mean that we may have neither your wealth nor my income when this thing is through. And even if we do, funds could be tied up, unavailable. For the present, I have only current rents. The men are being paid in paper money, 'shinplasters!' As for the future, everything is in question. We have no idea if this government is sufficiently stable to withstand an economic crisis. We have no currency. Adams founded the National Bank, and Jackson removed all the money. Van Buren is not doing anything, and the entire country is in depression."

Juliana turned to the window. Late spring in the city belied the grim nature of the conversation. Outdoors, a wealth of color and texture gave promise to the surroundings. The sky was deep blue with only wisps of clouds stretching toward the Sound. In silence, the couple absorbed the magnitude of the threat. Juliana moved to face David. "What will become of us?"

"Obviously, we won't be destroyed. I may have to work harder with our properties in the city, but we do own them. The other investments will come through the crisis with some value. In short, it will pass. But as of now, we must deal with it."

Julia remained silent during the exchange, thinking. She asked her father, "By being careful now, we may save ourselves greater hardship if matters get worse. Is that right, Papa?"

"You certainly have the essence of my direction, dear Julia."

***

At dinner, the silence was as thick as the slabs of roast. Julia, subdued by the knowledge of a family crisis, focused on her food without appetite. Juliana fussed about, serving the meal. David was preoccupied.

"Who will be at Gardiner's Island, Papa?"

"Sam and the girls. You do enjoy your cousins' company, don't you?"

Julia allowed her fork to pull a slice of meat from one side of her plate to the middle. "Yes, but . . ." She took a bite and chewed, creating a welcomed silence. When she had swallowed appropriately, she continued, "It's not the same. At Saratoga or Newport, we meet new people and have new experiences. Those places and the strangers whom we meet give us a different perspective. The island is like, well, home."

"You have objections to home?"

"Oh, Papa, that's not what I mean. I'm growing up, and travel helps. It gives me an opportunity to try—"

Juliana intervened, "A new persona."

Julia turned to her mother in admiration. "Exactly, Mama! How did you know?"

"I see it happening every day—Miss Julia Gardiner trying to determine who she is. With her father, she's a little girl. With her brothers, she's queen of the ball. With their friends, she's a flirt."

David smiled. "Well, Julia, the news isn't all bad. Margaret is coming home from school."

"Oh, Papa! Are we that poor?"

"No." David smiled at Julia's alarm. "She is very unhappy, and your mother and I feel that we can provide her education between us."

"Well at least Gardiner's Island will be tolerable." Julia breathed a sigh of relief.

***

Margaret was slim and slightly taller than Julia's diminutive five-foot-three inches. Her hair was auburn, lighter than Julia's dark curls. Her fair skin glowed. Once reunited, the sisters seemed inseparable. On a warm spring afternoon, they sat together on Julia's bed, talking about school.

Julia was calm, even philosophical. "Maybe you expected too much."

She searched her sister's face as Margaret vented, "I hated every minute of it." Her large eyes were flashing. "It felt as if I were in prison, or at least being punished. I'll never go back!"

"Did you tell Papa how you felt?"

"Of course . . . that's why I'm home. He will teach me French, history, and philosophy. I don't have to go back."

Julia leaned forward. "But didn't you have any fun?"

"Absolutely not." Margaret picked up a nail buffer that lay between them and turned her attention to her hands.

"No friends?"

Margaret sighed. "They weren't friends, Julia. They were paper doll playmates, all flitting about, talking about how rich and successful their fathers are and how their mothers are matching them up well. They don't know what life is all about."

Julia's expression suggested suppressed laughter. "And you do know what life is about?"

"Better than they do!"

"But what do we know, really? Anyhow, school wasn't nearly so bad for me. Maybe I'm just like your roommates.

We always managed to have a good time. Mrs. Chagaray didn't always like what we did, but that was her problem. I feel as if we taught each other more than the school ever did. We learned how to get along together and help one another, real stuff." Julia moved to the end of the bed and threw her legs over the edge.

Margaret followed her. "Maybe you had real people. I had mannequins. They taught me to be self-sufficient."

"I wonder if the difference between us is that you look for perfection, and I take what's there," Julia said.

"You make your own perfection!"

"What do you look for in friends, Margaret?"

"I don't know. Loyalty, support . . ."

"Perfection! See, I told you so!" Julia turned to Margaret and tilted her head to adjust to her little sister's new growth.

"Of course not! Nobody's perfect!"

"Except us!" they ended in unison, laughing.

***

Spirits were running high in spite of abbreviated vacation plans at the Gardiner household. The girls took pleasure in their shared activities. Their father, of course, kept up with the news. The papers were filled with the coronation of young Queen Victoria. Buckingham Palace was nearing completion. Every aspect of the royal life was a matter of grave interest to the young Gardiner girls.

Julia pondered, "I wonder if she will ever marry."

David's grin was hidden behind the paper. "At eighteen, I suspect she will. Ever consider heirs? I'm certain all of England will take an interest in her and her heir."

"Oh, my goodness, that's right. Her marriage will be a political affair. But how will she know if the man loves her?"

"Ask your mother."

"That's not what I mean. Not like you two. She's queen. Men will want to share, or worse, take over her power."

Juliana intervened. "That's how things happen with royalty, Julia. Might dictates marriage. The young lady may not have the opportunity to follow her heart."

"How terrible!"

David folded the paper and turned to his daughter. "Not necessarily, Julia. In other times all marriages were arranged. They turned out quite as happy or as unhappy as today. People should wed at their own social level. That restricts choice. They marry their own economic level, another restriction. Usually it is preferable to marry within one's own cultural milieu. See what I mean?"

"Really, Father, you make it sound as if girls were cattle being sold at auction."

"That's your description."

"Just don't try to auction me off!"

Chapter 5

1839

Julia's Indiscretion

Margaret knew something was amiss. The cousins, Eliza and Rueben Brumley, were visiting from the city. At dinner everyone was pale and tight-lipped. Julia, looking tearful, stared at her plate and was not at all conversational. Margaret had been isolated from her the entire day due to a lengthy meeting in Father's study, from which Margaret had been excluded and to which Julia had been commanded. Alex was frequently in this type of predicament. But neither David, the girls' younger brother, nor Alexander were home, and Julia was the one who seemed to be the center of unwanted attention.

Margaret was accustomed to being privy to Julia's every thought and action. And now, obviously, something was afoot, of which she had not been informed.

It was ten o'clock at night before she could contact her big sister. When she heard Julia return to her room from the lengthy confab downstairs, Margaret went to Julia's door and knocked.

"Who is it?" Julia sounded strange.

"Don't be silly. How many people are around here at this time of night? It's Margaret. Who'd you think?"

When Julia opened the door, Margaret's irritation turned to alarm. Julia was in her nightgown. Her hair was down and her eyes were red, as if she had been weeping for some time.

"What is it, Julia?" Margaret pushed past her and closed the door so they could speak in private. She expected the confidence that she was used to. "Everyone's been acting as if there has been a death in the family."

Julia started to cry again. "There has been a death—me!"

Margaret waited for her to say more. Julia wiped her nose on the sleeve of her nightgown, sighed, and said, "Remember about three months ago, maybe you were still away at school. Anyway, I went to the city. Eliza and Rueben invited me to go shopping for our vacation."

Margaret's alarm was now bordering on panic. "What happened?"

"Well before I went, I received this letter from someone at Bogert and Mecamlely's Department Store. A certain Mr. Evans said he noticed me while I was at Mrs. Chagary's, and he wanted to know if I was interested in 'public relations.' I couldn't imagine what he meant. But I was curious and bored."

Margaret's worst fears were calmed. Now, new ones replaced the original concern. "So . . . get on with it!"

"Well, when I visited the city to go shopping, I went to see Mr. Evans. We talked for a while. He explained that advertisement of the department store was changing. Women of fashion were now displaying the goods in tasteful advertisement. He assured me that I would remain anonymous. I couldn't imagine what would happen next, but I was safe. There were people all around, busy people who seemed to be doing important things. I guess they were putting flyers together. Anyway, we were in this big room with bright lights, and a backdrop that looked like a park.

"This man, Mr. Evans, gave me a dress to put on. He added a funny hat—the kind Mama's friends wear. It had an ostrich feather trailing down my back and over my shoulder. And he added a coat that had fur trim. He put an overcoat and a top hat on himself. Someone snapped a few pictures. I had what I thought was a purse, but it had writing on it. It said, 'I'll purchase at Bogert and Mecamley's, No. 86 Ninth Ave. Their goods are beautiful and astonishingly cheap.'[i]

"He took some more pictures, then paid me in cash twenty dollars! He told me that the pictures would be used in tasteful advertisements, and he said he hoped to see me again."

"What did Papa say?"

"I had no idea the pictures would be on every street corner in the city!"

"How did Papa find out?"

"It was in the newspaper, too."

The tension that had mounted now demanded release. Margaret started giggling, and Julia, too, needed relief. Her contorted face softened with a feeble smile. "Anyhow, I don't think it looks like me."

"Where is it? Can I see?"

Julia reached behind the chair and brought out the news-paper display: an image of Julia dressed in a fur-trimmed winter coat and a bizarre hat with ostrich feathers. She was on the arm of an older man, a dandy, also dressed in B&M clothing. On the handbag Julia carried was printed: "I'll purchase at Bogert and Mecamley's, No. 86 Ninth Ave. Their goods are beautiful and astonishingly cheap!"

Margaret gasped. Her giggles turned into substantial laughter. "But why in the world . . .?"

"I just needed to prove to myself that I was alive. Honestly, Papa doesn't know how dull it is around here. And now, even our summer vacations are gone!"

"It won't be dull for you when Father gets through with you. Sackcloth will replace fur and feathers."

"I'm already being forbidden trips to the city. And Mama's raving about how I've ruined our good name. We wouldn't shop there for anything!" Julia rubbed her eyes while Margaret, still looking at the paper, started to laugh again.

***

In the following weeks, with the improved economy and the relative security of the Gardiner income established, David Sr. started making plans for a tour of Europe to round the girls' education. Margaret complimented Julia, "Well, you certainly moved Papa to relieve our boredom!"

"He'll probably make me wear an iron maiden for the trip."

Margaret laughed at the vision of a cumbersome girdle. "No, he won't. But Mama may."

The girls shared hope that life would calm down and the trip could offer a return to normalcy. However, before that happened, Alexander sent a copy of the *Brooklyn Daily News* home. It was dated May 22, 1840. A certain Romeo Ringdove had written a tribute to the lovely lady on the placard at B&M's establishment:

In short, I was bedeviled quite,
Bewitched's a prettier word!
She stole my heart that luckless night,
This gentle singing bird.
She sang about "The Rustling Trees,"
"The Rush of Mountain Streams,"
"About the Balmy Southern Breeze,"
The "Sunlight's Radiant Beams" . . .

I grieve my love a belle should be,
The idol of each beau;
It makes it idle quite, for me
To idolize her so.
When gallants buzz like bees around
Who sweets from flowers suck.

Where will the man so vain be found
As hopes this rose to pluck?
And since, to end my cruel woes
No other model I see;
I'll be a hornet to her beaux,
To her a bumble-bee.[ii]

Before Julia and Margaret could devise a plan to show the offending publication to their parents, Eliza and Rueben once more appeared for a "visit." The girls waited upstairs in Julia's room for the summons that would call Julia to her father's study. They waited — and waited —

At seven o'clock the dinner bell was sounded. Fearing the worst, Margaret and Julia appeared together in the dining room. The four adults were seating themselves at the table. David was solemn; Juliana, tearful.

"Julia, I have bad news . . ."

"Yes, Father?" Margaret could not distinguish between her sister's effort to feign innocence and sheer concern. "What now?"

Silence.

"Ahem."

Margaret recognized her father's manner of stalling.

Julia repeated, "Yes, Father?" Her voice quivered.

"It seems one of your brothers' friends has made sport of your reputation. Read this!" He picked up the newspaper clipping from the table. The girls recognized the poem.

Julia took the paper in hand, read it, laid it on the table where Margaret could see and turned to her father. "Who did this?"

"We think a friend of your brothers, Alex or David, unless you know something we do not."

"Father! How could you?"

Juliana wiped a tear from her eye and said, "Don't blame us, Julia. You started this horrid mess."

Margaret said, "Mother, can't you see how hard all this is on Julia? She knows she's made a mistake. But you are treating her as if she lost her virtue instead of pulling a funny little prank."

"This is not a little prank!" Juliana put her hand to her forehead, and Margaret knew the migraine was on its way. The girls learned early on that a headache was the weapon Juliana used to deal effectively with crisis.

Julia straightened in her chair. "Mother, Father, I'm terribly sorry that I've caused you embarrassment. I know the whole thing has been awful for you. Apparently, either Alex or David—probably Alex—has made it worse by sharing with his friends. I can't do anything about that. But I do hope we can all see this situation for what it is. I'm not a lady of easy virtue."

Juliana gasped. "Really, Julia, don't make matters worse!"

"I haven't. I'm just asking that you do not blow the crisis out of proportion. This is an ill-conceived and rude message created by some idiot. But it is not the end of the world."

Juliana cried out, "But you may have ruined your chances for a good marriage, girl!"

"If the placard and this doggerel have ruined my chances with someone for a good marriage, then it wasn't that good a chance to begin with! I feel confident that my way in the world will not be shaken by this faux pas. I accept the chagrin, and wish to put it behind me."

David picked up his wine glass and toasted. "My eldest daughter is, belatedly, showing signs of good sense. Congratulations, my dear!"

Chapter 6

1839
John's Family Bliss

The next few years were peaceful and happy for John as a retired senator from Virginia. He made a profitable exchange of his property for a home in Williamsburg with more acreage. Soon, John was asked to run for a seat in the House of Delegates in Virginia. He enjoyed the trips to neighboring Richmond where he represented his neighbors. He was at home in the state Capitol tending to the affairs of the state. Politics occupied him, but did not detract from family life.

Robert, his second-oldest son, was home. Alice, Elizabeth, and Taz completed the domestic group. The girls helped their mother, studied French, and read. John oversaw Taz's studies. Taz particularly enjoyed science. John insisted upon careful consideration of philosophy and history. Robert read law and clerked for his father. The older boys were seeking their fortune away from the plantation.

John tried to maintain a reasonable distance from his sons' affairs, but he was increasingly curious about Robert's sudden attraction to serious drama. On a Sunday afternoon, while the men were sitting in the parlor, the aroma of dinner coming from the kitchen while Letitia and the girls were busy in the dining room, John carefully approached the subject of Robert's newfound interest.

"So, what play did you see in Richmond, son?"

"*Othello,* and the most wonderful woman plays Desdemona. She makes you feel her innocence and love, while Othello is burning with jealousy."

"Isn't she Thomas Cooper's daughter, Priscilla, and doesn't Cooper himself play Othello?"

"Yes, I consider it amazing that they play opposite each other so well."

John gave the situation some thought. "It seems as if Lear would be a more appropriate play for the two of them."

Appropriately, the Tyler family invited Priscilla to one Sunday dinner, and then another. Soon it became commonplace. John enjoyed her visits. She was at home with Alice and Elizabeth. He watched them chatting as they shared handwork. She enchanted Tazewell by finding his favorite topic and asking just the right questions. Such admiration persisted, even though Taz was at an age where girls were nonentities. Letitia also glowed at the prospect of her visits. The women bustled about the dining room discussing domestic affairs. John enjoyed the special form of tranquility the young lady brought with her. Robert showed an increasing sense of pride and determination as her visits multiplied.

Eventually, of course, her father was asked to join the family for a Sunday afternoon. John did not at first understand Robert's hesitancy at the suggestion, but soon after Robert asked for Priscilla's hand, the Sunday afternoon arrived when Thomas Cooper was to meet the Tylers.

Robert brought Priscilla and her father from Richmond. John and Letitia were standing at the door as they arrived. Robert helped Priscilla out of the carriage. After a pause, Robert got back into the carriage. Eventually a bulky and wobbly frame emerged, followed by Robert, who was supporting the gentleman.

My God, the man is drunk on a Sunday afternoon! John could barely absorb the information his eyes were supplying.

"Mother, Father, I'd like you to meet—"

Thomas interrupted, "The famous, the indomitable, the master of stage . . ." He bowed and nearly lost his balance.

Robert increased his support and continued, "Thomas Cooper."

John reached out his hand in greeting. Letitia curtsied.

Cooper turned his full attention to John. "Senator, I can't tell you how very much I appreciate your son. He's very good to my Priscilla, and she deserves a good man in her life."

As they moved to the living room, John, being temperate in his drinking habits, didn't know what to do next. Robert filled a brandy snifter and offered it to the guest.

"Dinner will be ready soon, Mr. Cooper. Would you like this until then?"

Tom grasped the glass. "Thank you, my boy. Thank you." He settled into a chair.

John seated himself uneasily across from his guest. In the silence that followed, John reflected on the many guests that had reclined in that seat—Henry Wise, of course, but others too: neighbors, occasionally a member of Congress passing through. Never in his memory had the chair been occupied by someone who was inebriated.

Across the room, Priscilla was standing, watching. Her face was impassive, but her eyes carried a message that John wanted to understand. They looked at each for several seconds.

Priscilla broke the silence. "He has had a very difficult life. Sometimes it eases the pain."

John studied her features and found a woman mature beyond her years, used to taking care of an ailing parent. He wanted to make the situation easier for her, saying simply, "I understand."

Dinner was served. Letitia was silent and looked down. Priscilla appeared somber; Robert, tense. John felt himself the host and wished to put the guests at ease.

"So, Mr. Cooper, you're spending some time in Richmond?"

"Ah yes, that community seems to appreciate our theatrical attempts more than most."

"Robert is our expert on the arts. He says your presentations are excellent."

"I'm afraid he is unduly influenced by my leading lady."

Robert interjected, "I saw the performance before I became an admirer. Don't forget the order of events."

Priscilla turned to John and said, "What is happing in the House of Delegates, Senator? Or is that all secret business?"

"Governance is never secret, my dear, and it is seldom interesting to women." John felt himself glow at the attention from this charming young woman.

Priscilla's eyes sparkled. "You never know, Senator. We are much more interested than circumstances allow us to show. And that interest is more widespread than most men care to see."

Robert interjected, "You certainly don't believe that women should be granted suffrage!"

"I believe we will vote one day. And I think we will make a significant contribution when that day comes. Until then, I'm willing to give my attention and advice to those of you who do govern." Priscilla placed her napkin on the table and turned to Letitia. "May I help you?" she said as Letitia rose.

Tom, Robert, and John returned to the parlor. The meal seemed to sober Tom. "My daughter is very outspoken. You will have to forgive her."

"That's an endearing quality." John passed the humidor to the other men and lit his cigar.

"Priscilla is a good girl. She has taken care of me since her mother . . . ah . . . left us. She couldn't take the life of the theater, you know. One day, she just packed up and . . . was gone. Priscilla and I had to fend for ourselves. Priscilla was only five when that happened."

John was curiously aware of Robert trying to decipher the feelings of the two fathers.

It wasn't until Robert returned from taking Tom and Priscilla home that he could talk to his parents. They were waiting for him. As he entered, he said, "Don't judge her by her father."

Letitia rose and went to him, kissing him on the cheek. "Robert, Priscilla is a dear. She has taken care of that man-child for eighteen years."

John puffed on his pipe. "Solid, that's what I'd call her. She has a lot in common with your mother, and she seems to know what she wants. I like her, Robert. I like her a lot."

The Tylers were soon making arrangements for a small but gracious wedding.

Before the big event, one night John's world was shattered. He was awakened by a loud thump and the sound of something—or someone—falling. At once aware that Letitia was not at his side, he rushed out into the hall, where she lay sprawled on the floor. John gathered Letitia in his arms to carry her to the bed.

"What is it, Father?" Robert rushed from his room. Taz and Elizabeth came into the hall.

"What's wrong with Mama?" Taz's voice was shaking.

"I can't tell. She seems to have fainted." John tried to stifle his own fear.

Robert dressed hurriedly to go get the doctor.

Slowly, Letitia regained consciousness. Something was terribly wrong. She was making unintelligible noises.

"Don't try to talk, my dear. It's too painful. The doctor will be here soon. Are you warm and comfortable?" Letitia's attempts to talk were unsuccessful. She started sobbing. He tried to calm her, not knowing if it was frustration or fear that moved her. "Rest now. It will be all right."

***

The doctor said she had had a stroke.

"It's too early to tell how much damage was done. She may recover completely, but residual damage to her speech or movement is possible. Or she may not remember. It is difficult to tell what functions are affected. Be prepared for anything, John."

The weeks wore on. Priscilla, now Robert's fiancée, spent time with the family. She was a calming influence, supporting John, comforting Taz, working with the daughters. John could feel her taking hold. Together they cared for Letitia.

John came into the bedroom as Priscilla was finishing Letitia's bath. He heard her say, "Now, Mother Tyler, you're fresh as a rose. Here, let me straighten your hair." She took the brush and ran it carefully over Letitia's grey locks. Letitia's eyes followed her. Slowly, she turned her head and acknowledged John with a small croak. Her eyes filled when she realized that she could not shape the words she wanted.

Priscilla walked from her to the window and back. "Don't worry, Mother, we will work with you and the speech will come back." She put her fingertips just below Letitia's jaw and pressed slightly. "Can you make a sound now?" Letitia complied.

John said, "Good morning, my love. You have the most wonderful speech teacher in the world."

Letitia pressed her lips together, "Priss . . . good."

"Mother, you did it!" Priscilla's acknowledgment of Letitia's achievement magnified the moment. She turned to

John. "Don't underestimate the effort that took on Mother Tyler's part. Finding the will to speak is one thing, but finding the mechanics—that's another story altogether!"

***

The family continued with plans for the wedding on September 12, when the heat of Virginia summer had passed. Letitia could not attend, but Priscilla and Robert visited her before the ceremony.

"I wish you could be with us, Mother." Priscilla was patting Letitia's face with a cool cloth. Letitia was unsuccessfully fighting tears.

"I . . . want to . . ." The remainder of her thought was lost in the immobility of the right side of her face. She turned her head.

"We love you. And we know you love us. You're going to be with us, really." She leaned over and gently moved Letitia's head so they could look at one another. "Thank you, Mother Tyler, for all you've done for me."

Letitia allowed tears to stream. She reached out with her good hand and took Priscilla's. Time stopped as they looked at each other. Priscilla leaned over and placed her arms around the fragile body, taking Letitia for the mother she never had. And, no less, Letitia took Priscilla as her daughter.

When Robert and Priscilla returned from a brief honeymoon in Baltimore, they settled in Robert's room. Priscilla proceeded to manage the household with an air of normalcy that comforted the Tyler home.

Chapter 7

1839

A New Political Overture

Although Henry Wise visited John frequently, he behaved as if he were unaware of the domestic changes forced upon the Tyler household. He came to talk politics. John knew to expect that. He detected a hidden agenda on this visit. Henry rocked in the chair opposite John, his feet not touching the floor when the rocker tipped. A cherubic face shone beneath baby-fine hair.

Henry smoked a cigar, laying it aside as he spoke. "You know, the Whig convention is to be in Harrisburg this December."

"The Whigs have no business having a convention. Conventions will lead to mob rule, and when you put all the Whigs together, they'll kill one another. Getting rid of Jackson—and now Van Buren—is all they have in common. They are like mad dogs: great for ridding us of something, but nothing pulls them together. It would be best to keep them contained."

"Now, John, a convention will be, and it must be. We've got to stick together. I think Henry Clay will take the nomination this time. The depression helps us, even though it seems to be slowly on the wane."

"Did Clay cause it so he would win?"

Wise ignored the obvious, ever-conscious of his own objectives. "He has the key to keeping this shaky Union just that, a union, in spite of people like Calhoun on one side and Webster on the other."

John smiled and retrieved his brandy. "He puts the two of them in a yolk and carries the whip himself. Sly, if not virtuous."

Henry thought a moment and said, "He needs Southern support, John, Virginia's especially. I don't know if Calhoun's Carolina will stay with him."

"You don't expect me to deliver this state to Clay, do you?"

"Just the Whigs, just in convention, just for now."

"The Virginia Whigs have no love for me. They are trying to keep me out of state politics this very minute. And there's the question of what Clay has done to the South."

Veins were beginning to show on Henry's neck. "There's no other way. We have to have a candidate, or there will be chaos in the country. The Whigs can win the presidency, but a fine thread holds them together. It is a shame we are in a depression, but the jobless in New York and Philadelphia will join us. Van Buren is part of the Jackson crowd, and they are out. They caused the financial crisis. We've got the election in our pocket if we have someone who can keep us together. Henry Clay is the man. Give him your best, John. You won't regret it. I need your word."

John did not answer. *My word is sacred. To promise this thing now is to support Henry Clay to the White House.* He raised his head, not looking at his longtime friend, but to heaven, as if in prayer.

"I need some time to consider, my friend."

***

Robert and Priscilla supported the idea that John go to the convention. They would care for Letitia and the children.

"Why you goin', Papa?" Young Tazewell was at John's side at every possible opportunity. He sought his father's constant attention since John's return, and Letitia's illness seemed to compound the boy's needs. John wanted Tazewell to understand the value of what he was doing and knew from his own childhood that the interest in political life needed to be fostered in youth.

"Well, son, the Union needs a good president, one that will bring us together. Mr. Van Buren has not done so well and he wants to try again, but we must find someone better. So I'm helping to look for the right man."

Letitia, in a rocker near the bed, checked buttons and worn places in Taz's clothing. Priscilla took items in need of repair. Letitia's slurred speech did not hide her thought processes. "You must do what is best for us all, family and nation."

John set the handkerchiefs in the bag he was filling and turned to touch Letitia's cheek. "I wish I could be certain what is best for the family." He looked at her and thought about the trip to Harrisburg. *I am going there to support Henry Clay, although I heartily dislike him. He can't be trusted. But my friend can be trusted, and he says that Clay is the only answer to Martin Van Buren.*

Letitia's fine-featured little face was somber. Her rare smile was awry. The paralysis affected her appearance.

Taz watched as Letitia continued, "You've never liked Mr. Clay, have you, dear?"

"Indeed, I do not. But Henry Wise indicated I have precious little choice."

Tazewell was sitting on the foot of his mother's bed. "I still don't understand why you're going. I know about Mr. Van Buren, but why Harrisburg and what about Mr. Clay?"

"Let's see—it's certainly easier to explain the convention than Mr. Clay. Until last election, candidates were named by state assemblies. But in 1835 the Democrats had a convention of delegates instead. In May, they had another one. And suddenly that's the way things are. Now, the Whigs must do the same. Last time, the Whigs had too many candidates because some states were traditional and others held conventions. Nobody quite knew who was on a state ballot or how they got there. The vote was split and Van Buren won."

"Was that when you were almost vice president?" Taz asked.

"That's right, son. Do you remember, or have you just heard us talk about it?" John looked at the youngster.

"I remember some, and I've thought about it some. If you'd been elected, would we live in Washington City?"

John laughed. "I don't know. There was only a slim chance that we would win, so I didn't think about it. Vice presidents don't have to live in Washington City. They don't really do much. Anyhow, this time the Whigs want to settle on one candidate and retire Mr. Van Buren." To Letitia, he added, "I wish it were that simple."

Letitia's mobile hand went to her throat where her lacy collar was in place. "John, you would make such a good president."

"No one is asking me to be president, dearest. Remember that I cannot garner enough votes to return to the Senate. Williamsburg seems about the limit of my constituency. And leaving you to go to Washington City would be even more difficult now."

"My problems can't stop your duties, John. Our country needs you." She became assertive. "If you are called to serve, you must."

"I'm called to be with you, love, and the children. It's good that Robert and Priscilla are with us. I can go as far as Harrisburg, offer my support, and know that you are in good hands."

***

Once at the Harrisburg convention, John was no more convinced of the wisdom of conventions—that newfangled system of choosing—than ever.

He argued with Henry Wise. "The Whigs have no business having a convention. Just listen to that pack. Conventions are the beginning of mob rule. That pack will kill one another. They are a group of mongrels with nothing in common. They are like mad dogs." John slammed his brandy snifter onto the table.

"It's too late to argue that, John. We're here, and we must stick together. I think Henry Clay will make it this time. Bad as it seems, the depression will help us."

"Humph! Henry Clay finally bought enough votes?"

"It's not like that. He has the key to keeping this shaky Union in a piece for a few years, anyway."

"Harrumph!" John retrieved his brandy.

"He needs Virginia. He can't win without this state."

"I carry no clout in this state. I'm accepted by neither Whigs nor Democrats."

"Clay has no loyalty, except to himself."

"We can win if we can stay united among ourselves. The Depression is terrible, but the jobless are with us. We can carry New York and Philadelphia—on the economy alone!"

"But we need someone who can keep us together. Henry Clay is the man. Give him your best. He needs Virginia, John. Please. I need your word."

John mused. The idea of Henry Clay in the White House was beyond terrible. *Give me time, Henry. You are asking too much!*

***

Henry returned to his theme that John support Clay. John's temperate manner was being pushed. "This issue in the House of Delegates is the last straw. They tried to bribe me—*me*, Henry. I can't believe their gall."

"I doubt that it came from Clay himself. He isn't much given to bribing anyone."

"When I asked the source of this tomfoolery, they said it was from the very top. Who else but Clay?" John rose to pace around the room.

Henry watched him moving around the room like a caged animal. "If Clay is nominated for president, no one from Virginia could possibly be named as vice president. It would be far too provincial. The industrial states would not tolerate it. We'd slit our own throats. Clay knows that, too."

"All I know is those damned Virginia Whigs collectively approached me and suggested that if I'd make no attempt to get a Senate seat, they would support me for president. I don't want the seat in the first place. But anyone who thinks I operate that way must be mad."

Henry blew smoke rings. "John, I know Clay well. He is smarter, cannier than that, believe me."

"The very thought that I may have to support that man makes me sick," John spoke though his teeth.

"Clay seems the only weapon we have in the battle against current chaos. The only other candidates are Winfield Scott, of dubious honor and less intelligence, and Harrison, who distinguished himself as an unsuccessful candidate last year.

You may remember the campaign, 'Log cabin and hard cider.' A real man of the people. Neither of those appeal, do they?"

***

In spite of Henry's ugly but impeccable logic, Harrison became the Whig candidate. The vice presidential office was tossed into the House of Representatives, where a Whig caucus settled on John to hold the South.

"Tippecanoe and Tyler too" became the by-word, and the campaign was in full swing.

Chapter 8

1840

Julia's Grand Tour

Although the country still felt the pain of depression, the Gardiner household's economic condition stabilized. David announced that a trip to Europe was in the works. As a result, the Gardiner home in East Hampton was bustling. Julia was occupied with wardrobe decisions, carefully chaperoned trips to the city for necessary accessories, trunks to fill, and French lessons. David booked the family on *The Sheridan*, due to leave for Europe on September 27. Before departure, he planned to take the family to Washington City to introduce them to the American political scene so that they would have a comparison to enhance their political education.

Julia read everything she could about Queen Victoria. The young monarch and her new husband, Albert, captured Julia's imagination. And now there were rumors that Victoria was in a family way.

"The next king!" Julia sighed, put the magazine down, and looked off into the distance. "I wonder if we will get to see the queen."

"Queens do not go around in public in her condition," Juliana said, "and I don't want you girls to discuss such matters around your brothers. It will embarrass them." She set her teacup firmly on the saucer.

Julia and Margaret shared a knowing glance.

Julia's excitement mounted when the family arrived in Washington City. It was a muggy September day. Although the train trip from New York City had taken twenty-four hours, the girls were far too enthusiastic to be tired. They settled into their suite at the Brown Hotel. Juliana retired to her room at once, complaining of a migraine, and asked for cool packs for her head. Her only comment was, "I detest this frontier town!"

David called for warm water, shaved, and changed. "I have an appointment at the Executive Mansion to see President Van Buren. The city is easy enough to manage; why don't you girls walk over there and look around? I brought you here to see and be seen, you know. We really should come when Congress is in session. You could watch the proceedings."

"What? A lot of old men making speeches?" Julia spit out the words.

"Important things happen that affect your life, my dear, and all of the men aren't old. Some are young and eligible." David straightened his tie and reached for his jacket.

Margaret said, "I don't want to marry a politician who makes speeches all the time."

"They do much more than talk. This is a center of power, where important decisions are made. I hope we will all become part of that process."

Julia crossed the room and further adjusted her father's tie. "I want to be the reigning monarch of some wonderful Shakespearian dukedom. I can escape to the Forest of Arden when my father becomes oppressive. He's a terrible dictator, you know, even if he does seem to be a sweet papa."

"No dukedom for you, young lady! You are in the middle of modern America, and you'll make your mark here." He picked up his bowler and walked to the door.

"Oh, Papa!" Julia ran after him and hugged him.

***

Julia and Margaret began their exploration by walking along the unpaved streets past the White House. "I think Dolley Madison lives over there." Julia twirled her parasol and pointed it toward a townhouse across Lafayette Square.

Margaret's eyes followed. "I wonder if we will see anyone famous or important."

"Papa is meeting the president. Is that important enough?"

"I thought he hated the president."

Julia flipped her parasol open. "Well we are in Washington City, and Papa has a way of going to the top."

"Just like you do, hmm, Julia?" The bite in Margaret's voice belied her role as a gracious younger sister.

Juliana joined the girls in the afternoon, saying she was some improved. They visited the Capitol.

"I do wish our capital city looked or felt like one," Juliana said.

Julia, charmed by her surroundings, said, "I like it here. It looks . . . well, fresh and expectant, like a lot can happen."

"It can't happen soon enough for me! I think my headache is returning. Ugh, the dust! It's indecent to have the capital of a nation look like a hick town on the frontier."

"But, Mother, it is a frontier town. All of Virginia is just to the west of us. And beyond that . . . well, who knows? The frontier!"

"Really, Julia, this is the capital! You just don't seem to understand."

"This city will be elegant someday. Just look at how the streets are laid out. It's as if we were going to have the whole world at our doorstep."

"I hope the whole world has sturdy shoe leather. These walks are terrible!" Juliana did not suffer discomfort gracefully.

Margaret said, "Mama, dear, you just have no spirit of adventure. What will happen when we go to Europe? We won't be in London and Paris all the time."

"It's civilized over there. There'll be more than the president's residence and the Brown Hotel! Wait until you see Parliament." She tossed her head in disdain toward the marble building behind them.

***

At the hotel, David joined the ladies over tea. Conversation again turned to Washington City social life.

"Isn't Van Buren a widower? Who's his hostess?" Julia asked.

"His daughter-in-law, Angelica, is the official hostess. I understand Dolley Madison is her cousin or aunt or something. Dolley all but arranged the marriage to Van Buren's son."

Margaret said, "Dolley must be a romantic."

Juliana poured herself a second cup of tea. "On the contrary—Dolley is a very practical woman who enjoyed running the White House social life and found a way to continue doing so."

"Really, Mother," Julia said. "You give no one any credit for good deeds. You always see an ulterior motive." Her voice was teasing.

"I'm an accurate judge of human nature. Dolley Madison gets what she wants. When Van Buren began to look like a president, she wanted several good social seasons. So she placed her ducks in a row and her niece in line. Other than Dolley, the women at the White House have been a sad lot for years now."

David said, "Oh, there have been some interesting characters in the mansion."

". . . But Dolley was the perfect hostess, to read about it. She knew just how to say the right thing to the right person, and there you are! A treaty signed, an ambassador in place— whatever," Juliana said.

"Abigail Adams was quite a rabble-rouser, wasn't she?"

"I understand Adams put the kibosh on her more than once," David said, laughing.

Julia was searching her memory. "I read somewhere that she wanted women to vote."

"Then her daughter-in-law, John Q.'s wife, was just the opposite. She's foreign-born and has a sense of where women belong," said Juliana.

David laughed. "I'll bet J. Q. reminds her where women belong, if she forgets. He reminds everyone else, including his fellow representatives. Probably treats her like he does Congress."

"Papa, is everything political?" Julia asked.

"Yes, my dear, everything is. You'll see!"

***

Later that evening, Julia and Margaret were in their room. Julia was staring into space.

"What is it?" Margaret asked.

"I was just thinking about Queen Victoria. She lives in splendor all the time, and she will have children who live in Buckingham Palace."

Margaret giggled. "I don't think President Van Buren will grace the White House with children."

"No, we don't have heirs to the throne. But I wonder how different royal life is. Victoria must love Albert."

Margaret sat on the bed next to her sister. "I certainly hope so. They are married!"

"Sometimes in royal marriages, love isn't even considered. They are designed to create allies and fend off enemies." Julia folded pleats in her navy blue dressing gown. "In one way that would be hideous. In another, it could be very exciting. It makes our lives seem so . . . well, purposeless."

Margaret studied her big sister. "Julia, your life will never be purposeless. And mine—ah—mine will be filled with true love, or . . . I'll just be your lady-in-waiting."

Talk of the campaign dominated Washington. The West, full of unknown quantities, was the area both parties wanted to control. David was full of political rumor when he returned from his visit to the White House with the New York delegation of congressmen.

"The Democrats want to embarrass this Tyler. They smell blood. They're asking him to describe his views on the National Bank. Ha!"

"What are his views?" Julia looked up from her diary.

"Well, he didn't think much of it in the thirties when he was in the Senate. So I doubt that ten years have changed his mind. The Whigs, so far, have answered for him. 'Mr. Tyler's opinions are already too well known through his speeches and votes. He does not need to respond.' I suspect the Whigs mean that it would be unwise to disclose his views in the face of a fragile alignment with the party."

"Goodness, Father, he sounds like a political misfit."

"I sometimes think the whole Whig party is just that: a misfit—or a collection of misfits."

"I can't imagine either you or Alex as a misfit in political circles." Julia's posture was erect, her diary next to her forgotten.

"These are strange times, Julia. Everything is in flux. The Whigs are a party of change at a time when we need just that. Harrison may be good for the country right now. Jackson's attitudes are getting old, worn out, and there's no going back to the days of Thomas Jefferson. So, maybe the way they forge ahead is right. Harrison doesn't say much, but he makes a good impression: quiet, but full of action."

"Maybe he makes a good impression because he's quiet."

David chuckled. "Astute observation, young lady. Have you been reading the papers?"

"Between you and Alex, I've decided that the politician who says the least is the best."

***

The Gardiner family departed Washington. In New York, they boarded the packet ship *The Sheridan* bound for London on September 27.

In their stateroom, Julia and Margaret were preparing for dinner that evening at the captain's table. Margaret, all dewy-eyed, asked, "Did you see him?"

"Who?"

"The captain, dummy, Captain de Pester?"

Julia had been considering more practical things, like how they would spend the next month in the space allotted them. The room had scarcely enough space for two cots. No mirror was evident. They each had one piece of luggage. The rest of their worldly goods were stored in one of the deep recesses below.

Margaret reminded Julia that as the oldest daughter traveling with the family, she would have the privilege of sitting next to the captain. "Please, Julia, you will have all kinds of chances to meet every man aboard. I'm a stepchild. Please let me sit next to him."

Julia felt very mature as she acquiesced to her sister's dearest wish.

At dinner, Julia made polite conversation with a shipmate on her right while watching her younger sister. The two-year difference in their ages could have been a full generation. Margaret was caught up in her flirtatious game. Julia, while discoursing with a handsome young man, was a million miles away, dreaming unformed dreams.

Julia enjoyed the first evening. But two miserable days followed. She did not appear for dinner on the second night and drank only tea on the third while seasickness took its toll. By the third evening, she was able to eat. And by the date of arrival in London, October 29, she was fully seafaring.

The Gardiners began a holiday in England, but politics in the States did not take a holiday.

Chapter 9

The Campaign That Wasn't

John was reluctant to involve himself in the campaign. However, he realized that some participation in the ensuing campaign was necessary. Reluctantly, he made his way to central Ohio to join in an activity for which he had no taste.

"These are our headquarters; a bona fide replica of the log cabin Tip was born in," the energetic young man from St. Clairsville, Ohio, told Tyler, who stifled the knowledge that Harrison was born in the manor of a plantation not distant from his own Greenway home. But that was only the beginning.

Through his friend Henry Wise, he was instructed to confine his words to the party line. He would have preferred to stay home, but an unusually successful campaign trip by his direct rival, Richard M. Johnson, caused a reluctant party to push him into a tour in the West. A direct question about a national bank caused John to deliver an elusive and clumsy statement: "There is not in the Constitution any express grant of power for such a purpose, and it never could be constitutional to exercise that power, save in the event the powers granted to Congress could not be carried out without resorting to such an institution."

He found himself very uncomfortable on the stump, saying nothing of importance and unable to move an audience that yearned for Tip's jovial personality. Fortunately, the attendees were content to sing, drink, and shout slogans.

Political audiences were new and different. Until 1840, men collected in smaller number to assure themselves that a candidate reflected their particular philosophy of government. Issues around the powers of the federal government verses those of the states dominated. This year, however, popularity with the voters seemed to depend on the ability of a candidate or his spokesman to entertain.

Tyler recognized himself as a student of governance, a thinker and legislator. His audiences seemed to demand an entertainer, leaving him baffled and uncomfortable. He recognized that he and Harrison agreed on very little, and Harrison was in the lead, so while he was tempted to challenge his own running mate, he withheld comment, making him a dry and insipid speaker in a situation that begged cause to cheer the hero and boo the villain.

Nor was he good at drinking whiskey, making small talk, shaking hands, and hugging babies; all tasks that seemed to be demanded of a candidate.

John was of another age. He considered this time immediately before election an opportunity to evaluate the incumbent's achievements and assets and to hear plans for the future. His biggest handicap was simply that no one considered a potential vice president very important, especially local politicians.

The meaningless words put into his mouth, composed by a campaign advisor, did not allow him to display confidence in the words he spoke. Try as he might, he could not control the tones coming from his own body. Then, when he introduced topics that mattered and he understood—the states and their rights within the Union, the danger of altering the relationship between levels of government, the nature of the Union—he saw his audience grow restless. People began to move away and look for drinks and entertainment. Hundreds of people who had come expecting to be entertained were bitterly disappointed. When he concluded, there was a bare minimum of applause. John knew his own failure. He couldn't find the chord needed to charm the crowds. And worse, he hated the whole circus mentality that surrounded an event supposed to be filled with dignity and deliberation. It seemed obvious that he was not at ease with men whose fingernails were dirty, who wore red kerchiefs around their necks where ties belonged.

Chapter 10

Julia Continues Her Grand Tour

From England, Julia learned about the campaign through David, who received letters and papers from New York sent by his son, Alexander. It was late afternoon when the family came home from a tour of London and Chelsea. David collected his mail and was sitting in their small parlor, reading snippets from Alex's report. He chuckled and then laughed out loud.

"In St. Clairsville, Ohio, Tyler absolutely tripped over himself, saying nothing. Listen to this." He quoted Tyler's less than lucid statement about the powers of the Constitution.

Julia had settled on the window seat to catch the last of daylight. She put her handwork down. "So, what does he mean, Papa?"

"He means, 'I hate the bank, and there will not be one, if I have my say. But Congress may feel otherwise. In which case, I don't know what I will do. But since I'm going to be the vice president, no one cares.'"

"So strange." Julia was pensive. "What will he do as vice president?"

"Not much. He presides over the Senate." David was reading, and now he burst out laughing. "Listen to this:

'Farewell Van
You're not our man
To guide our ship,
We'll try Old Tip.'"

Julia was laughing as she asked, "What's that?"
David read on,

"With Tip and Tyler
"We'll bust Van's B'[o]iller'"[iii]

Both girls were laughing now. "What in the world?"

"Those, my pretty maidens, are campaign slogans and songs. The whole country is full of them."

Juliana was looking out the window onto the London street. She said, "Well, that's certainly enough to make me glad we're here."

"Me too, Mama, but I do hope we will be able to see the queen." The youthful monarch continued to preoccupy Julia. "Just one glimpse . . ." she begged her father, who still occasionally seemed as if he could do anything.

As they moved through London and to the countryside, she began to give up hope of ever seeing the exciting young lady who ruled England. They were in the middle of an English winter with cold and dreary weather. Julia was affected by her mother's discontent. Juliana was unhappy, and she did not miss an opportunity to let her family know it. "There's little in London that New York City can't do better."

Julia thought of Buckingham Palace, Parliament, West-minster Abbey, the Tower of London, and the general air of antiquity that prevailed. And she remembered her mother's sound condemnation of Washington. She remained silent.

Margaret's romantic escapades had dominated the trip over from the States. Crossing the Channel, however, Julia once more took center stage. Sir John Bacon, a fellow traveler, appeared totally charmed by her grace and wit. They passed time on the deck together.

"I think I have learned to sail," she said as she inhaled the fresh, salty air.

"You make an exquisite sailor, mademoiselle."

"Why, thank you." Julia tipped her head in characteristic fashion.

Suddenly rain besieged the pair. Sir John pulled his mackintosh off and slipped it over Julia's head, then his own. For about thirty seconds she was grateful for the shelter, but very suddenly her stomach sent warnings that she recognized from her recent experience crossing the Atlantic. The odor of Sir John's cigar-filled breath and the oil smell from the mackintosh were too much. At first she ignored the warning, but as the nausea increased she found it necessary to hurry to the side of the deck. Her departure may have thwarted a romance, but she did not mourn the passing. She spent the remainder of the brief crossing in seclusion.

***

In Paris, David took Julia shopping for a guitar. They visited the shop of a craftsman. Julia could smell the fresh scent of wood recently varnished. She looked around to where stringed instruments in all stages of development were lying. The shop owner placed a guitar, finished and properly aged, in her hands. She began to strum, placing it close to her body.

"It doesn't feel right, Papa. It's too light, I think . . . no, maybe heavy, but in the wrong way." She furrowed her brow, not wanting to displease her father. "I want to keep the one I get forever. It's just got to be right."

"We'll find another." David thanked the shop owner, and they moved on to other artisans' quarters. Finally, in a small shop on a back street where the winter sun was streaming through the windows, the instrument maker placed a guitar in her hands. It was light wood, handcrafted by an apprentice. For Julia, it was love at first sound.

"Oh, Papa, this is the one!"

David gratefully completed the transaction and Julia had a guitar that she intended to keep and use forever.

"Now, young lady, this will have to be part of our luggage as we travel."

"Of course. I wouldn't trust it to be sent home. I will keep it with me always." The image of her stateroom on the return trip did not enter her mind.

On the way back to their rooms, Julia stroked the canvas that covered her new guitar. David watched with amusement that turned into curiosity. "What made you decide that was the guitar for you?"

"Well," Julia's look was pensive, "I just knew it. The weight was right. It's a little lighter than the others we saw. But mostly, everything just came together. It felt right . . . no, perfect."

David shook his head, watching her. "A lady that knows her own mind!"

"Oh, Papa, I'm not always sure about wrong things. But when something is right, I can tell!"

"I believe you can."

***

David looked up from the letter he was reading. It was shortly before Christmas. The family decided to remain in Paris over the holidays. The social season there would be the best possible exposure. "Are you ladies ready to go to court?"

Julia and Margaret ran to their father. "When, Papa? Oh, Papa, Papa, what will we wear?" The two spoke almost in unison.

David turned to Juliana. "My dear, I want the girls outfitted properly. I'm lending grace to the Court of France. I want those beauties fittingly decorated. But," he turned to the girls, "you must understand. The clothes are your Christmas presents."

"It's wonderful, Papa. We will have the best Christmas ever!"

The next weeks were spent in a flurry of visits to dressmaking shops, haberdasheries, and seamstress quarters. There was hardly time to eat and none to go sightseeing.

On Christmas morning, each girl discovered a small box on the mantle with her name on it. Julia received a diamond necklace. She opened the delicate card: *From Mother and Father, with love, Christmas 1840.*

"It's . . . beyond beautiful!" Rushing to a mirror, she laid it against the navy blue of her dressing gown. "It's perfect like a morning star!"

Margaret received a brooch with a similar diamond.

***

Dressed in the new French designer gowns, on February 7, they found themselves at court. The large drawing room was full of people like themselves, elegantly garbed and waiting with nervous anticipation for the royal couple to appear so that the festivities could begin.

"I can't believe we are here," Julia said.

"Why don't you find a count and marry into all of this?" Margaret asked.

"Why don't you?" Julia countered.

To a flourish of trumpet music, the double doors leading from the royal apartment opened and Louis Philippe entered. He was a short, stout, elderly gentleman in a wig of light brown hair, wearing the uniform of an army officer. The queen entered alone, capturing the undivided attention of the crowd. She was in red velvet. Her waist was cinctured with a band highlighted by a diamond clasp. She wore a headdress of diamonds.

The girls could barely see the royal pair passing through the throngs. "He looks old," Margaret said.

"But just look at how graciously he is greeting people!" Julia was drinking in every detail of protocol as the couple passed from one group to another. When they came to David, Juliana, and the girls, David bowed. Julia and Margaret curtsied.

Julia spoke to the queen in passable schoolgirl French with a dignity mixed with enthusiasm.

The king replied in his mother tongue and Julia made a discreet curtsy in response.

The royal couple passed along, talking to others, until at last they settled with the queen's entourage on a dais along the rear of the room.

"Look at them. I think she has chosen a court to highlight her own beauty." Julia was studying each woman. They sat surrounding the queen, but enough below her to demonstrate her superior rank. The white dresses highlighted the red of her gown. Julia stood in silent admiration.

Suddenly, a strange motion beside her demanded attention. She turned to see Margaret wilting at her side. She reached out just in time to break her sister's fall. Together, they went to the floor. Julia maintained a precarious balance and found herself sitting tall with a limp Margaret in her arms. Two pages rushed to her side and lifted Margaret's inert body.

Julia responded, *"Merci."* They moved Margaret, and Julia followed.

Settled in a spacious chamber with only the girls and the servants, Margaret came around. "What happened?"

"You tell us." The relief was evident in Julia's tone.

"It just got so warm, and all of a sudden everything turned black." Margaret started to sit up, and slumped back against the lounge.

The king entered, accompanied by a stranger. He introduced his personal physician to the girls. The king then instructed him to attend to Margaret. Taking Julia's arm, he returned to the main drawing room, speaking quietly to Julia.

As they passed into the reception area he said, "Mademoiselle, you deserve a palace in your future."

Julia was startled at the suggestion. "We live in a democracy, Your Highness. We have neither palace nor royalty."

"Nevertheless, you are deserving of royal treatment."

Julia curtsied and said, "*Merci*, Excellence."

The carriage ride in the dark winter night was silent. Everyone was exhausted. Julia broke the silence. "Nothing will ever be the same after today."

"Oh, I think it will. You may be different, young lady, but the world has not stopped because you were received at court." David's voice showed satisfaction that his eldest daughter was impressed as well as impressive.

***

The family visited Versailles. On the trip to the countryside, David reviewed the latest correspondence from Alexander on the scene at home. He wrote about Harrison's election and preparations at the White House.

"Does he say anything about Mrs. Harrison?" Julia asked.

"She's still in Fort Bend. She won't attend the inauguration ceremonies because she is preparing her household to move to Washington City later."

"I wonder why she isn't right there helping him now."

"Not every woman looks at Washington the way you do, my dear."

Julia turned to see the French landscape, but her thoughts were back home, where an inauguration would take place.

Chapter 11

Big Changes Everywhere

Tyler, out of courtesy, made plans to visit General Harrison while the president-elect was in Richmond. John found his suite and knocked. The general answered. The two men had met before, but had so little in common it seemed as if they did not know each other. After an awkward moment, the president-elect asked John to come in. He poured John some exquisite brandy, a French import. The two men attempted to make small talk.

"Webster to take state?" John asked.

"Mmm, I think George Badger will get navy. That should make your Southerners happy. And Francis Granger will be postmaster, Ewing for treasury; Bell, secretary of war, and Crittenden will be attorney general. That will complete my Cabinet. And John, you? What about you?"

"You will find me in the Senate, doing my best to make sense out of the affairs of the day. I certainly see no problem with your choices for Cabinet."

"We should do very well together." Harrison needed no more information. He seemed to settle down. He placed his cigar in an ashtray with the brandy next to it on the table. The silence became oppressive.

"Ahem, I must be going. I just wanted to wish you well and be caught up to speed. It's been good talking to you, Mr. President. Congratulations."

"Good, my man. We will see you at the inauguration?" Harrison didn't seem to wait for an answer. He rose and opened the door for John's departure.

***

March 14 was a cold, dreary day. John traveled to Washington reluctantly, wanting to return to Williamsburg as soon as possible. Just after noon, he was sworn into the office of vice president. He made a five-minute speech and prepared to fade into oblivion.

Harrison's speech lasted an hour and forty minutes. The rain stopped, but a brisk cold wind lashed at him and at his audience the entire time. The rain returned, and he stood in the pouring rain, assuring his fellow countrymen, "Freedom of the press is the greatest bulwark of civil and religious liberty." At sixty-eight, he was the oldest man ever to be inaugurated.

***

As vice president, John seemed functionless. He made no effort to move to Washington City, but remained at home tending his family and fields until Congress reassembled, when he would, reluctantly, chair the Senate.

Outdoors on that spring morning, April 5, John was on his way to the fields to direct the workers. Taz stopped him. "Father, how do you do a knuckle ball?" John looked at the lad with his tousled hair and large blue eyes that were pleading for companionship.

"Well, let's see. It's been a while, but . . ." He got to his knees, took the large agate marble in his hands, placed it between the second and third finger, and shot through the marbles, capturing a number of them.

He did not, at first, hear the horse and rider coming into the courtyard. He looked up to see the young man dismount. John held out his hand. The gentleman took it, then saluted smartly.

"Sir, I'm Fletcher Webster."

"Yes, yes, Daniel's nephew, isn't it?"

"Sir, the president is dead."

John looked at him in silence for a moment, then said slowly, "Then . . . I am the president?"

"Yes, sir, the interim president."

"The president, Fletcher. Check the Constitution's wording."

"Yes, sir."

"I must come to Washington." John was absorbing the implications of the news slowly.

"Yes, sir, I've come to fetch you back with me. If we can get to Richmond in time, we can get started for Washington today."

"Come inside and have a bite to eat. You've been on the road a long time. I'll pull a few things together and be ready within the hour."

Taz was standing at John's side. "Does this mean you can't play marbles anymore?"

John looked down at his youngest son. "That's what it means, boy." He dropped to one knee, bringing himself eye-level with Taz. "You have to look out for Mother, and pay attention to Robert and Priscilla. I need you to be a big boy now."

"Can I come to Washington City too?"

"Yes, you will follow me in a while. Right now, I must tell the family. This will mean a big change of plans. You will help me, won't you?"

Taz, having witnessed Fletcher's arrival, pulled to his full height and saluted smartly. "Yes, sir, Father!"

Chapter 12

Julia's International Romance

In Brussels, a handsome young count met Julia and paid her uncommon attention. They saw each other frequently. But Julia broke another heart because ". . . it wasn't right." Margaret looked on in dismay.

News of the death of President Harrison came by way of letter from Alexander. The event brought with it an official sense of mourning, but lacked any personal involvement. The girls appeared in formally proper mourning, with left wrists wrapped in black crepe. David mused with his family.

"Who is John Tyler?" Julia asked.

"Alexander said very little about him in the letter. 'In the midst of these scenes, Mr. Tyler has assumed the government and retained the Cabinet selected by General Harrison. Yet, some doubts are entertained whether he may not strike out a new course of political policy. The party insists that his opinions are now altogether Whig, and that he will carry out the measures proposed by the Harrison Administration.'"

The affairs of the States were set aside while the family visited Scotland and Ireland, where Julia met a Mr. Delebarger, a member of the War Ministry. He was fascinated by her. She was not attracted to him. At first, she allowed a flirtation. Soon, however, it became clear to her that his intentions were far too serious to trifle with. Juliana insisted she put a stop to the flirtation. Julia concurred.

Margaret asked, "What would you do if Mother tried that with someone you really loved?"

"She wouldn't do that if I really loved him. She would approve."

"I'm not so sure." Margaret had not had a serious conflict with her mother on the question of men, but a noticeable difference in values prevailed not only between the girls, but among the girls and their mother.

The Gardiners visited Vienna. While they were there, the Baroness Von Schmidt invited them to visit. The estate was outside the city wall in the foothills. Julia especially enjoyed the formal gardens, where she and Hans, the Baroness's son, were walking, as they had since the Gardiners' arrival.

"The climate is wonderful here." Julia was walking rapidly, breathing deeply, and drinking in the mountain view.

Hans, just behind her, watched. "You like my homeland?"

Julia turned to him and smiled. "I like your homeland, yes!"

"But do you like my home?"

"It's lovely." She looked again at the manor, now in the distance.

"Would you consider sharing it with me?"

Julia withdrew her hands from his and turned to the mountains. In silence, she slowly turned to him and said, "Isn't that premature?"

"In other circumstances, I would pursue a full-length courtship, but you are leaving soon. I would like a commitment before you return to America. We could arrange details later. May I speak to your father?"

Julia sighed deeply. She was quiet, reflecting on her own feelings. She thought she might be in love with him. Certainly she enjoyed a brief interlude when they first met, but in reality she hardly knew him. His proposal was a challenge. What would life be like away from New York, away from those she loved?

She turned back. "We will be here another week. I will give you an answer before we return to London."

After a concert at the opera house, Julia had a dream. She heard a great noise—thunder or wind. She saw balls of fire coming at her, black and white. She felt great joy and equal suffering. She must have cried out in her sleep, because Margaret was leaning over her. "What's the matter? Should I call Mama?"

Julia sat up and shook the sleep off. "I guess I was dreaming. I felt such . . . emotion, as if I were the happiest and the saddest person in the world, all at the same time. I felt as if my happiness was purchased at some great price."

"My goodness, Julia, even your dreams are exciting. Did it have anything to do with the baron?"

Julia was pensive. "He was not even an issue. He wasn't part of the dream at all."

"What if he really were serious, Julia?"

Julia faced Margaret squarely. "He is."

"Ooh!" Margaret clapped her hands together. "And you?"

"Until he actually approached me, maybe. But with an earnest proposal—well, no, it just wasn't there."

***

Julia was strangely preoccupied. "Papa . . ."

David put the letter aside. "What is it, Julia?"

"What would you say to Hans if he asked for my hand?"

Juliana asked, "Do you love him?"

David intervened, "Certainly not. How could she? They hardly know each other."

Juliana lay her hand on David's wrist. "Let the child answer for herself."

"I don't know. Sometimes I think so, and then . . . Well, I just don't know."

Juliana was firm. "Julia, if you have any doubt, you must delay. When you are really in love, you will know absolutely. Then nothing your father or I say will change your mind. So, as much as I would like to see you royally married, I do not feel the time is ripe."

David's tension eased. "Your mother is a very wise woman, Julia. Listen to her."

The Gardiner party found their way back to England, where they boarded the *Acadia* and left Europe to return home. They landed in Boston after a full year of travel to a country with a new president, one not elected to the office.

Chapter 13

John Is President

"John, for your inauguration—"

"There'll be no need for an inauguration, Henry. I'm the president. I became so the minute Old Tip stopped breathing."

"Don't get so almighty up in the air. No matter how you feel, there should be a formalizing, so that anyone who has any doubt . . ."

"The swearing-in would compromise my position . . ."

"John, you may be certain that you are president, but there are vultures out there who would like to keep you in a box. A swearing-in won't compromise you, it will demonstrate to your opponents—"

"No, Henry. I am the president."

"Do you expect Congress to agree?"

"Eventually, but not until I have affirmed the constitutional position on the matter."

"There's no precedent."

"I create the precedent. What I do now will be reflected for all time to come. The Constitution is clear, and it will prevail."

"The Constitution says the duties will fall upon you, not necessarily that you will become president."

"That is the precedent I intend to create. Henry Clay created this kettle of fish. Now I will make gumbo. When I was nominated, no one for a moment thought I would do anything but occupy the chair in the Senate. The speculators were wrong. I intend to be every inch a president. 'In the case of the removal of the president from office, or of his death, resignation, or inability to discharge the powers and duties of the said office, the same shall devolve on the vice president.' Do you remember?"

Henry turned his cherubic face up to John, who towered over him. "Don't expect everyone to agree. Please go through the ceremony. It won't affect precedent. What you do afterward will. A graceful concession on this issue will emphasize your position."

John's trust in his old friend prevailed. On April 5, 1841, at high noon in a small room at the Brown Hotel, Chief Justice William Cranch of the United States Circuit Court, District of Columbia, placed the Bible in John's hands and asked him to raise his right hand. The justice administered the oath of office.

***

The first encounter with Henry Clay was bound to be unpleasant. The issue of title, however, was resolved in John's mind.

The senator greeted him, "Good day, Mr. Vice President."

John's reply was terse. "I'm the president, sir."

Clay turned his back. John continued. "Senator Clay, if you have business with me—and I'm certain you must—perhaps you should get used to calling me by my proper title. I am the *president* of the United States."

John's reasoning was precise and legal. He was certain that his action on this matter would affect the Office of President for generations to come.

In the case of the removal of the president from office, or of his death, resignation, or inability to discharge the powers and duties of the said office, the same shall devolve on the vice president.

***

Henry Clay was not a man who surrendered power gracefully, especially when that power went to someone over whom he had no control. He persisted in the use of "Mr. Vice President" when addressing John or sending mail. John, in return, promptly sent all the mail back to the addressed, thereby depriving Clay of important opportunities to shape the events of the day.

Once John settled in the White House, Daniel Webster was among the first of his visitors. For all his formality, he was friendly, and he knew how to address John.

"Mr. President, it has been the custom of your predecessor to make all Cabinet decisions by a majority of that body." The information was delivered informally, as of little importance.

"What?"

Webster repeated his statement.

"Senator, I can assure you that you have described a custom that will not be continued. My Cabinet is composed of trusted advisors, but I am the president, and I shall be held responsible for my administration. I hold myself responsible." Thus ended the business portion of the Webster visit.

Later, John called the entire Cabinet together and again rejected the precedent set by President Harrison. "I shall be pleased to avail myself of your collective wisdom, but I can never consent to being dictated concerning what I shall or shall not approve. With that principle soundly in mind, I request all of you gentlemen to continue in the office you now hold. If you are willing to do so, continuity should be clear."

Chapter 14

Julia Goes to Washington

East Hampton was even more dull after the trip to Europe. Julia complained that she was dying of boredom. The courts of France and England poorly prepared the girls to bide their time at home.

With Alexander home at Christmas break, talk centered around Washington and politics. He spoke of Robert Tyler, son of the new president, and described the Whig uprising against the president to be caused by the bank problems. Julia was impatient with political detail. "Oh, Alex, tell us about the exciting things. What is happening at the levees in the evening and the teas in the afternoon? Who is seeing whom? Where is the scandal? But for goodness sake, do tell us about the president's sons."

Alexander was amused at the girls' preoccupation with trivia, but he had a wealth of such knowledge. "Well, Robert is married to a young lady who is serving as hostess in the White House. The president's wife is in ill health. I understand she had a heart attack or a stroke before the election, but the family chose to bring her to Washington when Tyler became president."

"Is Robert with the family?"

"No, at present he is in Philadelphia where he and his wife live. But she is in Washington, taking care of Mrs. Tyler, who is ill."

"It must be lonely for the couple, being apart, even though she's taking care of the president's wife."

"I don't know—the family members are close. They seem happy enough. There is a youngster—the youngest son of President Tyler. He's with them and seems to be enjoying the White House grounds. They all seem content. A couple of his daughters are with him. They are making the presidency a family matter. Goodness knows Tyler needs support. Neither party likes him, and the First Lady is ill. But he understands politics. He knew there'd be trouble when he ran."

"But does he understand women? I can't imagine being far from my husband like Priscilla is, just because my father-in-law is president." Julia paced the length of the room.

"Julia, dear, I cannot imagine a husband leaving you alone under any conditions. In fact, I have difficulty imagining a husband for you."

Later, Alexander spoke to David privately. "Father, the girls belong in Washington. The season is bound to be interesting. The president has a flock of youngsters. Robert's wife makes the most charming White House hostess since the days of Dolley Madison, and the grand dame herself dominates Washington social life. Young men who match the aspirations of Julia and Margaret are everywhere. The girls would cause a rage, I'm certain. This is a time of rapid change, and your presence in the capital would be a welcomed addition. There's the scent of men who want to make a differ-ence. The frontier fairly bursts with promise. People are moving out, pushing limits. Every day the actual size of this land is growing. The split between the South and the North is growing and must be addressed by strong men of reason. Abolitionists are growing in number, and Southerners are becoming more entrenched in states' rights oratory. A cool, dispassionate head to talk to both sides, start a dialogue between the sides, and to settle disputes could do much good right now."

David listened carefully and thought for a few moments. "It is time I start thinking about Julia's future. I wonder if Wash-ington is the place to have her meet . . ." His voice trailed off.

Alexander grinned broadly. "Finish your thought, Father. You want both of them to marry well, don't you?" David nodded. "Staying in East Hampton means we must import any potential suitors. If the girls are in the capital, they can make choices from eligible young men. It is not manipulative. We aren't setting them up. They are so independent. I suspect any suitor either of us offered would be immediately rejected. In the capital, they meet whoever . . ."

David eyed his son, speculating. "I wouldn't want to manipulate their future, but . . ."

Alexander concluded, "Exposure does assist their choices of good matches. You would meet Dolley again. She is a born matchmaker."

***

As the train moved south, January weather changed from the snow they left in New York and into a drizzling rain in Maryland. The girls looked out the window until the car door opened. Only Julia could see the young man entering. Margaret's back was to the door. He looked at Julia and nodded. She dipped her head slightly in response as he passed her and greeted David cordially.

Margaret whispered, "Who's that?"

"I don't know, but I think we may find out. Father is bringing him to us."

"Girls, I'd like you to meet Congressman Fillmore from Buffalo." David nodded toward the tall man with sandy-colored hair and a charming grin.

Fillmore took Julia's hand and kissed it ceremoniously. Then he turned to Margaret and bowed deeply. "I'm charmed. Washington will be graced by such beauty."

Julia, enjoying the attention, replied, "Why, thank you, sir. Certainly the frontier has its own beauty."

David interrupted, "The congressman has suggested we might take rooms at Mrs. Peyton's, where he stays."

"Your family will be a welcomed entourage there. Also, I will see that Dolley knows you are in town."

"Dolley Madison?" Although Julia was incredulous, she maintained a calm voice.

"Yes, the reigning socialite in the capital. She will probably have you engaged to an ambassador before sunset. And if she can, she will see to it that every single congressman meets you, to say nothing of senators and judges."

Margaret commented, "Mother says she is a romantic. You seem to confirm that judgment."

"Dolley is a wonderful old dumpling. You will love her from the first draw of snuff."

The girls raised eyebrows. He continued, "Oh, prepare yourselves. She is unconventional, but has a heart of absolute gold. Well, nice meeting you. I trust we will see more of each other."

As the door closed, Margaret asked, "Is he married?"

David laughed. "Indeed, he is. Furthermore, I don't think the frontier life would agree with you. But don't worry; Washington is full of appropriate suitors."

Fillmore's major contribution to the Washington adventure was the suggestion that they settle at Mrs. Peyton's, a boarding establishment on the corner of Pennsylvania and Fourth and One Half Streets. David acquired quarters there. Other boarders were Francis Pickens and Thomas Sumter from South Carolina and Supreme Court Justice John McLean.

***

The family settled in their rooms as a messenger arrived with Dolley Madison's card and a handwritten note: *Please don't stand on formality. Come on Wednesday afternoon to visit. I am eager to get to know the family.* The card was signed "D. M."

At the appropriate time, Juliana accompanied the girls to meet the grand dame of the city. Julia was dressed in a yellow gown of empire style, a soft low-cut neckline, a high waist, a flowing skirt, and a bustle. She was wrapped in a cape. Margaret wore a smart blue pelisse gown and a coat.

They knocked and were admitted by a servant who took their wraps. Almost before Juliana had her coat off, a small puff of feathers, bows, and satin came rushing up to them.

"You must be the Gardiners!" She reached out to hug all of them as they turned. Julia responded warmly. Margaret froze as the little elf reached for her. Juliana quickly held out a gloved hand to forestall any more intimate contact. Dolley responded to each in kind, unaware of any hint of rebuff.

"Come with me where it's comfortable. We must get to know one another." She led Julia by the hand. The others followed.

Julia was aware that the supple, warm hand had a surprisingly strong grip. She moved in unison with the hostess-whirlwind, wondering what else was in store. Margaret glanced back at her mother, whose face was frozen in a kind of disdain.

The drawing room had a warm fire, and the library table was filled with serving pieces: a samovar, sugar bowl, creamer, and a pitcher with hot chocolate. French pastries laden with icing were on a serving dish near the beverages. The Gardiner women moved to the chairs and settee that surrounded the fireplace. In the background, winter sun was streaming in the frosted windows.

"I've heard so much about you. Millard spoke highly of you, and Robert Tyler knows your brother. He said you were coming. I'm so glad. You will brighten everything."

Juliana replied, "The girls are looking forward to the season."

When they were settled, the servant appeared and passed cups of chocolate and a tray of rich confections. Dolley continued, "You must visit Congress. The galleries are wonderful places to see what is happening and meet the men who are making it happen. I take a group over there whenever Congress is in session. Of course," she giggled, "I am privileged to sit on the congressional floor, but we all hear the same thing."

Julia had a fleeting vision of this little lady literally sitting on the tiled floor, but she said nothing. Margaret saved the conversation. "That must be quite an honor, Mrs. Madison. You certainly have earned it."

The women sipped chocolate and heard about all the eligible young men in the capital. "My niece, Angela, married one of President Van Buren's sons. She was the official hostess at the Executive Mansion, since the president was a widower. Angela's marriage was actually in the White House."

Julia found her enthusiasm contagious. She asked questions unabashedly. "What's the White House like? Is it impressive? We've been to Europe, you know. It is like foreign capitals?"

Dolley wolfed down a second pastry, licked her fingers, and said, "It had just gotten to where I wanted it when the British burned it down. After the war, I had a terrible time. We had to replace everything. Since then, very little has occurred. Thirty-five years have taken a toll. Congress won't appropriate a cent for President Tyler to improve conditions. Mr. Clay fights President Tyler at every opportunity."

As they were leaving, Dolley issued another invitation. "I'm having a few friends in tomorrow night. Please come and bring Senator Gardiner."

Juliana and the girls thanked her.

***

At home that evening, Margaret was moving idly about from bed to window to dressing table. Julia was sitting on the bed, buffing her nails. She said, "What did you think of our hostess?"

Margaret stopped and turned. "I don't know. My first impression was how ugly she was. But before we left, I came to see her as radiant. She has so much . . . charm."

Julia looked up. "That's funny. I was amused at first, but never did I see her as ugly. She has goodness and eagerness written all over her. I just want to know her better. I suppose Mother was horrified at her manners. Imagine, hugging us upon meeting!"

"That's Mother's conservative nature. I love Dolley already, and we've only seen her once."

Chapter 15

John's Problem: Clay Is Not Malleable

Abel Upshur, a friend, called on the president to congratulate him. "You know the waters are shark-infested, don't you?"

"I also know the sun sets in the west." John turned to the window. "Yes, I've got Clay men, Webster men, Harrisonians, Old Whigs, New Whigs, Southerners, and Northerners. All of them want something, but my choices are limited. The less I upset matters, the better chance I have of gaining sufficient ascendency to keep the country running, and eventually of setting a course of direction that I choose. Therefore, I'm retaining Harrison's Cabinet—for now."

Upshur rose and shook John's hand. "I have great faith in your judgment, John. I hope that you aren't being too optimistic in your evaluation of these men."

"That is a risk I must take, Abel. Loyalties will work themselves out. I will win some, and I will probably suffer losses." John opened the door and showed his friend out.

Harrison's funeral was April 7. Tyler planned his inaugural address for April 9. Among his few friends— Upshur, Henry Wise, and Duff Green—John relaxed and considered strategy.

"I wonder if it might be best for me to follow Old Tip's example and make it clear at the outset I will not run for reelection."

Duff jumped to his feet and paced the floor. "No, Mr. President. That, decidedly, is not a good idea. It would be an immediate display of weakness. It was when Harrison did it, and it would be even worse for you."

The others affirmed Green's assertion.

"That's an ace in your pocket. You've got to hold onto it," Wise said. "You may even change your mind."

Upshur added, "Yes, John. Don't burn your bridges. It may take more than one term to settle issues that are important to all of us."

John developed his address to point to the depressed economy as being much in need of attention. He avoided banking issues, suggested no specific changes, reaffirmed his faith in the Constitution, and proposed to move ahead within the limits thereof.

Getting along with Henry Clay occupied much of John's thinking. He was especially sensitive to the implications of the Bank and Clay's attitudes. John gave careful consideration to a solution to the dilemma. Finally, he invited Clay to the White House, taking the initiative, in order to make peace and find a compromise.

Clay listened, showing no emotion, until he asked, "A banking bill, then, would be approved by the White House?"

"By the president? Yes, Senator, I could approve one that did not violate my sense of constitutional limitations on the federal government."

"Would you consider making such a request of Congress when you address us?" Clay seemed calculating.

"I believe I mentioned that I'm not enthusiastic about such a plan, but I do hope we can meet on common ground. I will see what I can find in my heart to say."

Clay ignored the reluctance and replied, "I shall expect to hear, then, that you wish to see some legislation on the matter and will be open to acceptance."

After Clay took his leave, John realized that he had not once used John's proper title.

***

Later, Clay was talking to his friends. "The man's an ass. He talks constitutional this and that, but he did tell me that Congress could design a financial weapon and he would approve it."

"Or veto, if he doesn't approve," Henry Wise corrected.

"I'll worry about a veto when it happens. After all, I have his word, and if he breaks it . . ." Clay's voice drifted off as he made plans. Possibly he could have what he wanted and draw blood at the same time. The title of president for John Tyler was out of the question.

***

John hoped his message to Congress on the subject of a bank was tactful. "I will entertain the possibility of a financial institution for the United States. Congress must reject any measure which conflicts with the Constitution, or otherwise jeopardizes the prosperity of the country. I will look favorably upon a suitable fiscal agent capable of adding increased facilities in the collection and disbursement of public revenues. The system must, however, be void of offense to the Constitution."

It was only a matter of days before the ghost of this peace offering began to haunt. The special session opened. Tyler and Wise assessed support for Clay's position. In the House there were 122 votes for, and 103 opposed to, the National Bank.

John studied their calculations. "His real problem is that Clay confuses the party and himself. It looks as if I may have an opportunity to assert leadership."

"You must be very careful, John. Just because those men oppose the Bank doesn't mean that they support you."

"Clay's demands reflect his own sentiment. They are not what Congress wants."

John offered Congress a compromise. He asked for a system where a bank would be incorporated by Congress in the District of Columbia, under the provision of the Constitution that empowered Congress to legislate for that area. The Bank could then establish branches in states, but only with the state's consent.

"I hope that will satisfy Clay. He gets his bank, and I have a shred of the Constitution left."

Clay, the great compromiser, was in no mood to compromise on this issue.

Tyler submitted his bank plan to Congress. Clay's committee, however, offered a counter-proposal that did not require the states to agree to banks in their territory.

John and Henry Wise studied the latest version of the bank bill. "It is the power to create a corporation that will operate in every state; that's the contest. That's Clay's assessment. Certainly not all the Senate agrees. And I can always veto!"

Henry looked up from the offending paper. "Be careful, John. A veto this soon after taking office over something this important could be very harmful to you."

"I'm not here to win a popularity contest. I'm here for the good of the country."

"Just be careful."

The committee offered a final version of the bill. Now, the matter of participation was voluntary. However, there was an assumption of approval if no objection was expressed during the first session following the passage of the bill. Once established, a branch could only be removed by consent of Congress.

These qualifications pushed John's tolerance beyond the limit. The Cabinet met. Seated around the conference table, they discussed the proposal.

"It gives you what you ask for, Mr. President." Webster sat nearest John. His usually assertive voice was soft.

Bell said, "I think you should accept the bill as it is. You've made your point."

Crittenden's voice now turned threatening. "You can only push so far, sir. The opposition will begin to push back."

Webster was listening carefully, weighing each comment. "The final decision will be yours, sir. Be certain you weigh all that will follow against any weakness you perceive in the bill."

After the Cabinet members adjourned, John recalculated the risk with Henry Wise. "I'm tired of placating Clay. I've tried over and over. And this is his idea of compromise."

Henry's forehead wrinkled. He paced nervously. "John, he's come a long way on this issue. You do have a consent clause in there."

"It's hidden!"

"He gave you what you asked for."

"I want sovereign states. He gave me a cumbersome institution that circumvents sovereignty."

"Compromise, John."

"When you compromise too much, nothing is left."

"The price of veto is high."

"Henry, sometimes I think you know the price of everything and the value of nothing."

"If you can reconcile this bill to yourself, all is sunshine and calm. Your administration will be met with the warm, hearty, and zealous support of the entire Whig party. When you retire from the great theater of national politics, it will be with the thanks and plaudits and approbation of your countrymen."

"I will go to church on Sunday and earnestly pray for enlightenment."

On April 16, John vetoed the bill presented by Congress.

Whig members of the Senate reacted violently to the veto message. They were betrayed. Clay let them believe that John had given his word. He did not apprise them of the changes his committee made unilaterally.

Democrats, on the other hand, appreciated the veto. It conformed to their understanding of the Constitution, but John was a Whig. His defection from the Democratic Party was a sore spot. They remained hostile, scared from the last election.

John did receive some support. At a session in the House, speeches reviling John as an upstart pretender to the presidency, a monarchist in disguise, and a rogue prevailed. One voice of support was heard in support of John: "Arrest the bank ruffians for insulting the president of the United States!"

Coming from Congressman Benton, that was praise indeed.

***

That evening Thomas Benton, Buchanan, and Calhoun, not notable friends of the president, but Southerners who recognized a victory, called on the White House to congratulate Tyler on standing by principle. Priscilla was hostess. Drinks were served, easing tension. The brandy aided, and the party turned from formal to jovial.

Priscilla went upstairs to check on Letitia's wellbeing. She returned looking concerned and called John aside.

"Father Tyler, there are demonstrators outside. They have guns, but their bugles and drums are more offensive. Mother Tyler is terribly upset. She can hear the noise. Fortunately, they are out of her sight."

John excused himself and went to an upstairs window, where he could see the demonstration. "This, my dear, is the price we must pay for protecting the Union as I see fit." He turned to Priscilla. "Keep Mother as far from the noisy side of the house as you can."

He returned to his celebrating guests, much sobered.

"Gentlemen, we may have won the skirmish this afternoon, but there are battles yet to be fought. Not everyone agrees with our stance."

The next morning, John discovered evidence that he had been burned in effigy outside the White House.

The following week, Clay, president of the Senate, officially demanded that Tyler "accede to the will of the nation or resign as president."

When John heard of the speech, he simply said, "He sometimes confuses the will of the nation with his own will."

Clay's attacks were a minor disturbance compared to the vitriol John endured from his friends. When John Botts turned on him, John knew he had trouble within what he had previously considered his own ranks.

John described the situation to Robert. "He actually accuses me of going back on my word at Harrisburg and on the campaign trail."

"Well, did you?"

"Son, you know me better than that. Of course the party leadership suggested I not be too forceful on the issue, or for that matter on any issue. But at no time did I paint myself into a corner where I would have to support any bank legislation the Whigs threw at me."

Robert thought for a moment. "What'll you do now, Father?"

"What I've always done—just keep going. I have another veto in the wings. The Fiscal Corporation Bill is coming up, and that won't get off my desk with approval. The whole crowd will holler like stuck pigs when it happens again. Unfortunately, the Cabinet put this legislation together. I think Clay put them up to it. I didn't see the proposal until it crossed my desk after passing both houses. Henry Wise tried to modify it so I would be saved embarrassment, but to no avail. Clay thinks I will be forced to sign it since the Cabinet members are virtual sponsors."

John Crittenden hosted a dinner party to which Tyler was invited. He declined. Pressures from his growing difficulty with Congress and the personal problem of his ailing wife caused him to decline the invitation.

The party was a gala affair, and liquor flowed generously. A group of Tyler's friends were named to go to the president and command his presence. Henry Wise led the delegation. They were received at the White House.

Tyler acknowledged them and said, "Gentlemen, what can I do for you?"

Wise took the lead. "Mr. President, we do truly need your presence at the Attorney General's home to make our evening a success."

"You know, Henry, sociability does not make me a mellower student of government theory."

"No, John, but it might prove to some that you do not have horns. Come back with us, please."

Tyler agreed, reluctantly.

***

When they arrived at Crittenden's home, John was greeted by Henry Clay, who offered him whisky or champagne. Tyler accepted the champagne. Clay began a recitation of Richard III, directed to John:

> *Let not our babbling dreams affright our souls,*
> *Conscience is but a word that cowards use*
> *Devil'd at first to keep the strong in awe.*[iv]

Tyler was silent. He looked long at the senator, and then turned to his host. "Sir, I do not miss the connotation." To Wise, he said, "Is this why you brought me out of my home?"

"It's the real world, Mr. President. You live in it."

"And I make decisions in it. I make them in the light of the best conscience I know, Henry, and I shall continue to do so."[v]

"The issues at hand now, Mr. President, will either yield you a strong following and a healthy Whig party, or will wreak havoc on the nation. For if there is no Whig party, then there will be no other voice."

"Your message is clear. Thank you, gentlemen. I value your advice. But I must sleep with my decision."

***

Tyler's veto message offered his constitutional objections to the latest fiscal corporation. The reaction to the veto was swift and uncompromising.

John Junior knocked on his father's study door. His face was strained and sad. "Your Cabinet is here, Father."

"I didn't request their presence."

"I know, but they are here."

"Show them in."

Five men walked into the room: Thomas Ewing, Secretary of Treasury, John Bell, Secretary of War, John Crittenden, Attorney General, Francis Granger, Postmaster General, and George Badger, Secretary of Navy. Each was holding a sheet of white paper. John sensed the contents.

"Mr. President, we have been given no choice but to resign. We feel that we executed your mandate in the manner agreed upon and submitted it to Congress, who produced legislation that conformed to your wishes. We have been publically embarrassed and repudiated. Your veto denies us confidence we need to serve adequately." John Crittenden was the spokesman for the group.

"Your decisions are final? Thank you, gentlemen. I shall not trouble you further." Each man handed John his resignation and walked out. He stood at his desk and stared at the resignations.

Young John knocked and then entered the study. The president spoke first. "Maybe it's just as well. They were neither my friends nor my allies. Now, I can appoint men whom I can trust, and the business of government shall continue."

"It won't be easy, Father."

"No, but something will occur to lighten the load."

Tyler now sat in the executive chair, lacking counsel. Democrats had not elected him. Whigs deserted him. Two days later he was formally and officially expelled from the Whig party. Seventy Whig congressmen caucused in Capitol Square and in all solemnity repudiated Tyler.

He was now, truly, a president without a party.

Chapter 16

Julia and Washington Society

David and Purser Waldron escorted the ladies to Dolley's evening gathering. Gentlemen in stiff collars and formal black coats stood in small groups. Women's gowns filled the room with bouffant sleeves and hooped skirts. Dolley was dressed in a cerise gown with a full bustle. Her turban matched. She looked like a small ball of fire as she introduced the Gardiners to Washington City's elite.

"And I'd like you to meet Congressman Caleb Cushing from Massachusetts."

"Charmed." Julia held her hand out to the tall congressman with burning eyes.

"As am I." There was a significant pause before he greeted the rest of the family. Julia watched Margaret's reaction to the young man as she curtsied slightly and held her hand out, observing him closely.

Cushing greeted everyone and turned his attention to Julia. Supreme Court Justice John McLean walked up to the group. "I see my fellow occupants of Mrs. Peyton's have found their way into the social strata. How nice to see you here."

McLean was of medium height with dark hair carefully combed to conceal thinning. He had a Virginia accent, in contrast with Cushing's clipped Massachusetts speech. He and Cushing exchanged greetings. McLean said, "You will have to join us at home, Caleb. The Gardiners are accomplished musicians. We have delightful concerts in the evening."

Caleb turned to Julia. "I certainly hope to see more of you."

"You are very kind, sir."

***

Soon, the evenings at Mrs. Peyton's were as interesting as the outings in the town. A few minutes after dinner, the men adjourned to the sitting room for a smoke and the women to the drawing room for casual conversation. After an appropriate delay, a gentleman would appear at the door of the ladies' parlor and suggest a whist game. Julia and Margaret, who tired of women's company easily, cheerfully joined the gentlemen and whist began.

Cushing, with his straight, lean figure and Massachusetts accent that spoke of culture, frequently requested that Julia be his partner.

However, Francis Pickens was also attentive to the Gardiner women. Neither Julia nor Margaret ever lacked a partner. Both were reasonably well-versed in the game of whist, having played it for recreation while in school and at home, especially on holidays and when visiting cousins.

When the invitation to visit the Wickliffe family arrived, Julia and Margaret carefully prepared for the occasion. Margaret, dressed in a corselet and pantaloons, was fussing with the crinoline petticoats. "What was the naval officer's name, the one Dolley recruited to escort us?"

"Richard Waldron. He's from New Hampshire and he's a purser in the navy. I adore him. Richard and Colonel Sumter are going to take us to the Wickliffe's."

"Who are the Wickliffes? And how on earth did we get an invitation?"

"I suppose our fairy godmother arranged it. Wickliffe is postmaster general. I guess he has daughters—girls, like us." Julia, brushing her hair, stopped and looked in the mirror. She arranged her flowing locks carefully over her shoulders and turned to catch her side view.

"I'd like it better if he had sons." Margaret waited for her turn at the mirror. She had her hands on Julia's waist, where the petticoats emphasized the narrow contour.

"There will be other men there. We have an advantage with Mr. Sumter and Purser Waldron. Besides, sport is no fun without competition."

Margaret snapped, "Friendship is not a sport!"

"Oh yes, it is, where men are concerned."

"Julia, you can be so cruel!"

"Don't take life so seriously, little sister. The solemn days of maturity will overtake you soon enough. Enjoy!"

***

After their visit, Margaret was much more enthusiastic about the Wickliffe girls. "They are so real. I think we will enjoy their company.

"Tomorrow, Dolley will take us to hear the debates in the House of Representatives," Margaret finished the thought, "and then the Senate."

Julia giggled. "Yes, but Dolley will be sitting on the floor!"

***

It was a grey afternoon. The girls had no plans; an unusual situation. David, Margaret, and Julia were in their sitting room. Margaret asked David a general question about the tension between the states. He responded with a general answer concerning the varying attitudes toward "that peculiar institution." David described the economy of the Southern states' dependency on slaves, and he emphasized that states' rights could not be abrogated by a federal form of government. Margaret reflected on the relative comfort and ease in the lives of the slaves they had witnessed while they were in Washington. It seemed to contradict much that was written in Northern newspapers.

"I don't see what the problem is, Papa."

David put his newspaper down in order to fully engage with his daughters. "Well, the problem really exists on two levels. One is constitutional, in that it designates that a slave is three-fifths of a man. That figure gives the South a bit of an edge when we are choosing leaders, but I don't think that's what the hue and cry is about. The complaint seems to be treatment of the slave problem. What we've seen in the South doesn't leave much room for that argument.

Servants are servants. They are fed, housed, and clothed. They work for their living, and they are protected as long as they live useful lives and obey civil and moral law."

"But that's just like at home, except our help lives away from us. I haven't seen anything in the South that distinguishes their culture from ours." Julia was thoughtful, searching her memory for a wrinkle in what she viewed as normal.

David was thoughtful. "I'm not sure there is much difference. But we don't live in the South, and we know only the more cultured levels of society. There may be more dissension than we see. And probably all is not this calm where there are agitators."

"Why would anyone stir up trouble?" asked Julia.

"You're talking human nature, dear. And I believe there are instances of rank injustice that we've been spared seeing. Of course, there's talk of equality, but that's a chimera any way you look at it. There are levels of education and culture that divide people everywhere. It's next to impossible to change that and never possible to erase the fact. Some of us are born with more of everything that adds up to station than others are."

***

The Wickliffe family entertained frequently that spring. The Gardiners, by now the toast of Washington, were invited. On an ideal spring evening, the air was heavy with the scent of flowering trees. A mild breeze came from the

Potomac. In Wickliffe's manicured yard, tulips, daffodils, and hyacinth were in full bloom. Tables laden with food and drink were tended by bustling servants. Judge McLean entered, escorting the Gardiner girls. Nannie and Mary Wickliffe greeted the trio as they came into the yard.

"Oh, Julia, guess who's here?" Nannie, the eldest daughter of the postmaster general, was a tall, redheaded girl. Her laughing eyes and dancing voice made her seem like bubbly wine.

"Well, it's hard to tell." Julia placed her hand on McLean's arm. "When a member of the Supreme Court brings you to a party, other guests pale in comparison."

McLean patted her hand. "Kind of you to say so, Miss Julia, but not true."

They turned back to Nannie. Margaret asked, "So, who?"

"The president's son, Robert. He's visiting from Philadelphia."

Just then a stranger, medium-tall with blond hair, a very friendly smile, and blue eyes that hinted of good humor, walked up. The judge said, "May I present Robert Tyler."

"And we were just now hearing about you." Julia held out her gloved hand.

Robert took it and kissed it gently while looking steadily at her. Margaret received the same greeting. "You are recently returned from Europe, I understand."

Julia's voice danced. "Oh yes, we visited England, France, Italy, and Austria."

"Did you find it strikingly different from our country?"

"It was mostly that we are new, while they are old. Wouldn't you say, Margaret?"

"There were manners and custom, protocol and . . ." Margaret's voice trailed off.

"We were glad to be home!" Julia added.

Margaret said, "It's best to be where you understand not only the language, but also the manners and customs."

Robert turned to the younger sister. "And you understand Washington?"

Everyone laughed as Margaret blushed. "Well, I understand Americans—at least some Americans."

"Ah, Miss Margaret, wait until you've seen more of our capital. You must translate the language of the frontier in Congress. They don't speak English in Kentucky, and congressmen from Maine don't know what Virginians are saying."

Judge McLean said, "Oh, it's not that bad. You are just sensitive because you work among the immigrants on Philadelphia's dock. No one understands them."

"On the contrary, they learn to speak our language rapidly. Their main goal is to be assimilated. They make wonderful citizens."

McLean acknowledged Robert's point and excused himself, leaving Robert with Nannie, Julia, and Margaret discussing the vagaries of Washington.

Francis Pickens, a representative from South Carolina, was among the frequent attendees. He was very attentive to Julia. He was a Southerner through and through, gallant, and restrained when in the company of women. His presence at social affairs was duly noted by the Gardiner sisters in spite of the fact he was reputed to be a widower with four children.

Pickens joined the small group around the president's son and greeted the women. "I trust you young ladies are enjoying your stay in our fair capital?"

"Oh yes, sir." Margaret was beaming. "You play a great game of whist, although I hardly get to enjoy it when I'm playing against you."

"You are a formidable opponent, Miss Gardiner. I can hardly judge my own aptitude when I'm in the company of the famous Gardiner women." He turned to Julia. "How do we in the United States compare with Europe? Were you spoiled by the standards of antiquity?"

"Not in the least, sir. We were very happy to be home and to return to Washington City, where all the real energy of the country seems centered."

"Oh, ma'am, you should visit the South. There is no city quite like Charleston to exemplify the real South."

"I'm sure, sir, but right now we have our hands full with our mutual capital. But, undoubtedly, the day will come when we experience your famous Southern hospitality."

Representative Pickens persisted in his attention to the Gardiner women. When on a subsequent day they attended a session at the Capitol, he carefully escorted them to their seats and then, rather than take his own place on the floor, he sat between Julia and Margaret "in case you have any questions," he assured them.

The threesome settled to listen to the business at hand.

After the assembly adjourned, Pickens escorted the Gardiners home, attending to their every need. At the door, in the fashion of a Southern gentleman, he kissed each girl's hand and bowed ceremoniously.

***

That night at Mrs. Peyton's, the girls were preparing for bed.

"Oh, Julia, the president's son! Isn't he wonderful? I was so overwhelmed; I couldn't even talk, but you engaged him." Margaret was brushing her hair. She gazed into space as she put down the brush.

Julia picked it up and continued to brush Margaret's hair. "He seems very intelligent. He was interested in our trip to Europe, so he was easy to talk to, really."

"I hope we see him again."

"We will. I'm sure we will."

"Did you hear that awful man from the Russian Embassy?" Margaret said as she turned to face Julia. "People don't say things like that about an ambassador's wife. Wars have been started over less."

"Really, Margaret, you are making too much of it. Congressman Ward simply observed that the wife of the Russian ambassador wore a gown that clearly demonstrated her physical beauty. She left little to the imagination."

"But people in the diplomatic world just don't say things like that!"

Julia leaned over to look squarely at Margaret. "Or maybe they do. I say, we have a lot more to learn about this city."

***

The two representatives at Mrs. Peyton's might have been matched bookends. Both were tall, over six feet. Both were gracious. One, Caleb Cushing, was from Massachusetts. He was soft-spoken. He had dark curly hair that would not lie in place, giving him a boyish air. Julia was impressed with his wisdom, and often consulted him on matters of the day. Francis Pickens, also tall and dark, was a representative from South Carolina. He had a gracious air. His manner was courtly. He was well-versed on political issues, but Julia was never completely at ease with him as her mentor.

"He seems as if he is trying to sell me something," she told Margaret as they analyzed the people with whom they shared family meals and evening recreation.

"His Southern accent is charming," Margaret said. "But Mr. Cushing is, well, I don't know. He's just dreamy."

The two girls were sitting on the bed playing *Pease Porridge Hot*. Only the chant and the sound of their clapping hands were heard at first, then laughter. "Well, if you want to give up your rights to Mr. Cushing, just let me be the first to know," Margaret said.

"I don't have any rights . . . What about Mr. Pickens?"

"Goodness, Julia, he's said to be a widower with four children. I don't think I could handle that."

"I don't think I could either. Just imagine becoming a mother to someone else's children!"

Chapter 17
John's Tribulation

John stared out the window. A wave of loneliness swept over him. He had no Cabinet, no advisers. The newspapers denounced him. Clay was furious, behaving like a raging bull. Even friends were distancing themselves as if he had the plague. Young John, now the president's secretary, knocked, opened the door, and announced, "A visitor, Mr. President," then retreated hastily. A figure appeared.

Although he was not large, the man filled the doorway by sheer force of energy.

"Mr. President." Daniel Webster's voice was deep and rich, commanding attention with the simplest phrase. He alone had not walked out on John's administration.

John had not fully appreciated that fact until this moment. "Come in, Daniel."

Webster slowly and deliberately closed the door behind him. John was aware of his penetrating eyes and the power they seemed to possess.

"Where am I to go, Mr. President?" Webster's voice acted as a magnet, drawing John's full attention. John allowed the significance of the question to sink in. Webster was an ambitious man who knew that anyone who aligned himself with the president would incur Clay's wrath.

"You must decide for yourself." John moved across the room, nearer to his visitor.

"If you leave it to me, Mr. President, I will stay as I am."

"Give me your hand on that, and Henry Clay is a doomed man." With this single ally, John could regroup, restructure his forces, and continue to govern. "You know there will be repercussions?"

"Repercussions are the result of significant action, Mr. President. I have a good bit of experience at state. I feel these items should be attended to, and I am well able to do so. The political climate changes from day to day."

John pulled two chairs out from the conference table. They discussed the English treaty concerning the Northern border.

Webster rose to go. "Thank you for your courtesy, Mr. President."

"Mr. Secretary, thank you for your confidence." The two men shook hands.

John felt twenty years younger when Webster departed.

***

Whig newspapers maintained a barrage of bad press, saying that Tyler bit the hand that fed him. "Betrayal" of the Whigs was playing havoc with his creditability. Democrats were silent. They could not be expected to come to his aid.

Even in the areas where they might have given support, they refused to acknowledge John's wisdom.

Attacks on the president were so personal and vitriolic that they could not be mentioned upstairs where Letitia was dying. In other circumstances, John would have shared and she would carefully listen and admonish him to follow his conscience. But he could not burden her with the petty hatred and vindictiveness that he faced.

His son John acted as his personal secretary and maintained order. More importantly, he shared his father's concerns.

"Your mother should know as little of these unpleasantries as possible. It is difficult to keep bad news far away when ruffians and rowdies stand outside and make noises that would wake the dead."

"Mother is certainly in no state to hear this nonsense."

"Poor Letitia, she knows so little of evil. I don't know what she would make of these times. How do you explain men like Henry Clay or his pack of thieves to a saint?"

"Well, Father, you have me. We have always agreed that I do understand thieves and scallywags. And Priscilla is here. It's too bad Robert is so firmly entrenched in Philadelphia. He enjoys the political fray more than I do."

John mused momentarily. "He does a good job of political organization. Because of him, I probably have more immigrant support among the dock workers in Philadelphia than I do here in Congress."

The young man's laughter was tinged with cynicism. "You have more support almost anywhere than you do here."

***

John spent more time with Letitia as she lay dying. Each day he was at her bedside. Frequently, she was sleeping. But on this day she was fully conscious, even talkative. They reminisced.

"Only yesterday, I wanted to help you so much. Remember Williamsburg?" From her pillow, she smiled.

He chuckled. "We managed a lot of joy, even in those tiny quarters. When Mary was born, we hardly knew where the next meal was coming from. Your father was right to reject me. I did not provide very well."

She reached for his hand. "Nonsense, I had all I could want. We never missed a meal."

"Only because you learned early to stretch everything, to make do."

"We were rich in love, John. Take care of the children. Alice and Taz still need you."

"They all do. Yes, dear, I do try to be a good father."

Letitia moved her partially paralyzed but still peaceful face to see him. "John, when two people truly love each other, they are never gone from one another. Don't forget that when I'm gone. I'll be near, looking for your happiness."

When she did die—late in the afternoon on September 10, 1842—she died peacefully, without fear, a rose in her hand.

Priscilla, the faithful daughter-in-law, was out of town visiting her sister when Letitia died. *The Washington* described

Letitia as "loving and confiding to her husband, gentle and affectionate to her children, kind and charitable to the needy and afflicted."

John's grief was silent. It started the day of Letitia's stroke, but he had memories to help him heal. Their five-year courtship when her family was reluctant to accept him, as he had few resources, was bittersweet. Along with her fierce loyalty, there was her gentle good humor to ease every situation. Even when she was too frail to stand with him, she continued to support him by her love. They were best friends. Her death brought with it a sense of peace, with memories of a wonderful and durable fabric of life that was his time with Letitia. But closure came with it. He was very much alive, and lonely.

It seemed to John that nothing could repair or rebuild his life. He'd lost his life partner. He had no political base, children to raise, and a country to lead that did not wish to move in a wise direction.

Chapter 18

Too Many Suitors

The grey days of December 1842 were brightened in Washington City when the Gardiners returned. The girls quickly paid a visit to Dolley.

"Margaret, Julia, I'm so glad you are back in town. Social life has been as dull as the weather." They were standing in the spacious entrance hall at Lafayette Square as Dolley ran to them. She was wearing a turquoise dress with a low-cut, square neckline where a suggestion of lace attracted the eye. She took their coats and turned to the maid. "Bess, dear, be sure these dry while the girls are here." The servant took the coats and Dolley led them to the library.

Settled in front of the fireplace, chocolate drink in hand, Dolley turned to local news. "This town is lonely—actually in mourning. We didn't know how much the First Lady influenced everything until she died. Now the crepe in the mansion, the lack of entertainment—it all lends itself to making Washington a place of mourning."

"We've read about it, of course, but how was it really?" Julia set her cup on the table and leaned forward.

"Well, you know that she was ill even before she came here. Her death was quiet. She lay in state in the East Room, and a committee, which I chaired, of the citizens of Washington City accompanied her casket from the Capitol to her final resting place. She's buried in Tidewater County, you know. The city bells tolled. It was the saddest sound. People cried and sobbed as she was buried. She was a quiet lady, like a small, grey dove; she brought peace wherever she went."

"How sad, especially for the president."

"It is. He was very close to his wife. He depended on her in any number of ways. Now he's torn between duty and his grief. Priscilla continues to manage official duties, but there is certainly no gaiety in the White House—only duty."

***

Young John Tyler paid his respects at Mr. Peyton's one evening. Of course, there were no official functions at the Executive Mansion. Otherwise, social life picked up exactly where the girls left it.

David called on the president. As he rose to depart, John said, "Do bring your family over for a visit. I'm not doing any official entertaining, but the girls, Taz, John, and I could use some good company. "

David held out his hand. "That sounds wonderful, Mr. President. We will do that."

"Good, maybe tomorrow night?"

David's surprise was poorly concealed. "I'm afraid we have other plans. But such a visit would be great. All of us would enjoy meeting your family. I believe our girls are about the same age."

The president smiled pleasantly. "Excellent. When the opportunity arises, I shall greatly enjoy a quiet and informal visit. Have your daughters bring their musical instruments."

David smiled. "My wife opted to stay in New York. She does not take to extended travel well. Julia and Margaret both play musical instruments. Margaret plays the piano. Julia is quite a virtuoso. We provided her with a guitar while we were in Paris. When she plays, you'd think she and it were one."

John chuckled as he opened the door for David. "We will supply the piano. Do have Miss Julia bring her guitar. I shall add my violin to the ensemble. A gathering of families sounds wonderful."

At home, Julia asked, "Who was responsible for our invitation?"

David said, "I believe I am responsible for that, my dear. The conversation was between the president and me."

***

After dinner, Caleb Cushing invited Julia to go for a walk. The weather was mild; one of those deceptive days that promises the coming of spring, when the wise know it is not yet. The pair strolled along Pennsylvania Avenue.

"Miss Julia, I am about to go to China. The president has appointed me as a commissioner to do some negotiation."

"How exciting! I'm impressed, Mr. Cushing, and we shall miss you."

He hesitated. "Ah, that is what I want to talk to you about, Miss Gardiner. Would you consider coming with me, as my wife?"

Julia stopped short. "Mr. Cushing, I hardly know you."

"We would have a good life, some travel. I feel that you would fit into the diplomatic work very well. And I do believe I'm in love with you."

She turned her head to hide her confusion. "No, no, Mr. Cushing. I couldn't."

"Will you consider the matter?"

"Please, don't . . . well, don't count on it. I don't know my own feelings. And . . . no, I can't. Your request is very flattering, but I'm not ready."

The two returned to Mrs. Peyton's with Julia flushed and confused; Cushing, subdued.

***

Francis Pickens played whist regularly with the family at Mrs. Peyton's. Not long after Cushing's proposal, Pickens invited Julia to go walking. They passed the White House, chatting casually. Suddenly Mr. Pickens stopped, turned to Julia, and ever-so-gently turned her to himself. "Miss Julia, it would be a great honor if you would consider marriage."

Julia looked up as if she didn't understand him. He seemed to be speaking in a foreign tongue. "What?"

"I'm proposin', Miss Julia. I want to say up front that I have four children, but you would not be burdened with them. They have excellent care and will be off to school very soon. Our life could be . . . just fine. I can offer you security and seasons here in Washington, and I would enjoy a—" He blushed.

"What, Mr. Pickens?"

"I'm afraid it's very bold of me. You are so young and energetic and all. I started to say I could handle more children, because I . . . you will . . . I don't mean to presume. But I am deeply in love with you, Miss Julia. Would you consider marriage?"

Julia turned from him, gaining time to frame her answer. "Mr. Pickens, I do not want you to have false hopes. No, I will not marry you. I value your friendship, but I simply am not in love with you. Please don't think me ungracious. I can only answer your lovely proposal with complete honesty."

The solemn pair returned to Mrs. Peyton's.

***

When Margaret heard about the Pickens proposal, she seemed hurt and angry. "Honestly, Julia, I do wish you appreciated your gifts. Francis Pickens is a wonderful man. And you just brush him off!"

"Well, he's too intense for me. He's . . . well, I'm just not ready to marry. I've only begun to live, and besides, there are the children."

Margaret relented, "Well, in his case, I should be slow to follow you and pick up the pieces. But if Caleb Cushing ever . . ." Julia looked away. "Julia, has he?"

"Yes. He's going to China. He asked me to come with him. I didn't want to tell you . . ."

"For fear my feelings would be hurt?"

Julia reached out to touch Margaret who seemed so vulnerable. "Your time will come with all that's happening here. These men know I'm ripe for picking. Your time will come. You are still young."

"There isn't that much difference between eighteen and twenty-one."

"Yes, there is. There's a world, Margaret, you'll see."

"I'm not like you, Julia. I don't flirt!"

"But when you want something, or someone, you know how to go after it—or him, don't you?"

"I only know how to be myself."

"That's all it takes."

Chapter 19
Julia Visits the White House

The evening of the White House call, Julia was carefully dressed in burgundy velvet with a wide lace collar that framed her face. Pearls laced her dark hair. On one hand, she chafed under the weight of her father's words about Washington. On the other, she was taken up with the sheer grandeur of being a visitor at the Executive Mansion.

They were admitted by a servant. John greeted them in the hall and ushered them upstairs to the family quarters, where John Jr., Priscilla, Alice, and Taz were waiting. The president introduced his family, and everyone settled on the aged, ragged sofa and chairs. Cordial and biscuits were served.

Julia liked Alice at once. She asked, "Do you attend school here in Washington City?"

Alice was petite, dressed in navy blue with a starched white collar and cuffs. The accessories accentuated her schoolgirl appearance. She had fair skin. Her eyes were highlighted by the blue.

"No, I stay in Virginia with my sister, Elizabeth. But I want to be with Father over the holidays, this year especially. Taz stays at Elizabeth's too." She turned to her little brother. "I think Father wants him near while the grief is so fresh."

"It must be very difficult—"

Julia's words were cut off by John. "Do you think you could add a modest violinist to your ensemble?"

Julia was taken by surprise. "Do you play, Mr. President?"

"Some, when I can." John went to the mantle and picked up his instrument.

Julia reached for her guitar and took it out of its case, while Margaret settled at the piano. Together they tuned the strings. As the mixed tones created a mellow effect, the trio fell naturally into "Open Thy Lattice to Love." They moved to folk music and solos for the violin and then piano. Julia's mood rose with the sound. She smiled and looked up at John. "That's wonderful."

He looked at her and beamed. "Chords from heaven."

***

The evening was apparently a success, because the president sent a message requesting that the Gardiners join his family for an informal celebration on Christmas Eve. This gathering was small by Executive Mansion standards, but larger than the earlier gathering. Purser Waldron escorted the girls. He was relieved of Julia's company when John greeted them and moved her away. They entered the Red Room, done in Florentine style. The deep red upholstery was worn and stained, and the gold leaf was peeling. Most of the party remained standing.

Julia looked around. "See Colonel Sumter? Who is the couple talking to him?"

"That's Mr. and Mrs. Robert McClennan. He's a congressman from New York. Congressman Richard Davis is with them. He's from New York, too."

"I know Davis; he lives at Mrs. Peyton's." Just as Julia spoke, the congressman detached himself from that group and approached John Jr. and Julia. Dolley came right behind him.

Davis said, "Good evening, Miss Julia. I didn't know you would be here. We could have shared a carriage." His cravat seemed oversized, as if his chin would fall into the great gaping hole it created and he might disappear.

Dolley burst into the conversation. "See, I was right! You girls add sunshine wherever you go. Even this sad old place is better because you are here."

"Hello, Dolley," the girls said in unison. David bowed and kissed the dowager's hand. Young John Tyler joined the group, standing near Julia and laying a hand on her arm.

Julia turned to him and, returning to the original conversation, said, "I was just telling the congressman how Purser Waldron takes charge of us when Father is busy." She turned from Dolley to Davis. "But thank you for your offer. Possibly another time." Ending that exchange, she turned to young John. "Does Priscilla plan these events?"

"Yes," he nodded toward Dolley, "with Mrs. Madison's help. They seem to thrive on the social calendar." Davis' head bobbed from John to Julia and back again.

"And your wife?" asked Julia.

John did not meet Julia's eyes. "Well, Mattie and I are not together at the present time."

"I do hope matters clear up in the near future." A subtle change in Julia's posture created a formal distance between the two.

"Thank you," he said.

Julia carefully included Davis and Dolley in the conversation. "Time does wonders. It is a natural balm."

Dolley commented, "That's what I've told the president."

John Jr. said, "Yes, I can honestly say that work has helped my father greatly. It keeps him going, and every day it gets easier."

Dolley said, "He will be his old self again before long, I predict."

Julia looked thoughtful. "I doubt that one ever really gets over the loss of a spouse."

Dolley said, "When my Jemmy died, I thought the world came to an end. But it didn't. I found that out when I discovered that I had to scratch to find my next meal. So, I learned to get on with life. The president will do the same."

John Jr. looked down at Dolley as if searching for a clue. "I'm sure you are correct."

Toward the end of the evening, the president approached Julia. He bowed and took her hand. "Miss Gardiner, I'm delighted that you chose to spend Christmas Eve with us." He did not let her hand go.

"Thank you, Mr. President. It's an honor to be here. This season must be especially difficult." Julia could feel his eyes, as if they, too, were holding her.

John did not move. He spoke softly. "Losses are very much a part of life. The pain I feel is the result of a close relationship.

I consider myself fortunate. The sorrow I now bear is a small price for our life together. Letitia was a wonderful wife."

"You have a fine family, too." Julia could feel herself blushing. She made a gentle attempt to remove her hand. The president resisted. She acquiesced.

"I'm glad you like them. I hope we will see more of you."

"Thank you, Mr. President." Julia started to curtsy. The president's hold of her hand did not diminish. She looked at him, and he at her for a long moment. She was sure her face matched her dress now.

John broke the spell, but still did not let go of her hand. "May I show you around?" He placed her hand on his arm and led her from the Red Room to the hall and into the State Dining Room. She looked up at the elaborate crystal chandeliers and at the long mahogany dining table.

"This must be impressive when you entertain dignitaries."

"The whole place badly needs a coat of paint, and this room, no less. But the furniture here does not deteriorate as quickly as in the sitting rooms, so it maintains some dignity. Come, there's more to see." They passed the Red Room and the Blue Room, where the hum of conversation could be heard. Downstairs, they entered the library, softly lit be a single gas lamp.

She examined the artifacts that were accumulated by the previous occupants. The magnetism of the presidential home was compelling. Yet more, she felt a magic that she could not define. She turned to John. "Should we rejoin your guests?"

John was silent. He looked at her for a long moment. "They don't miss me. I've planned it so they entertain one another."

Julia moved to the door. "Possibly, you underestimate your absence. We should find out."

***

When the Gardiner family made preparations to depart that night, the president again approached Julia, and took her hand as he spoke to David. "I hope you and your lovely family will join us again soon."

"Thank you, Mr. President. It would be a pleasure."

David held out his hand. The president turned and kissed Julia delicately on the cheek before responding to her father.

***

The following Sunday, Juliana insisted that Julia stay home in bed while the rest of the family attend church. "Listen to you! You're honking like a goose."

Julia sniffled, and turned to go to her room. "I don't feel good. Maybe it's just as well."

"Of course it is. Who ever heard of a debutante with a runny nose! You need rest to get over this thing."

David, Juliana, and Margaret arrived at St. John's Episcopal Church a few moments late. It was crowded. They tried to be inconspicuous as they entered. When the president saw them, he rose from his seat near the front of the church. The remainder of his row was empty. He bowed to David and motioned for the family to sit with him.

When they returned home, Margaret related these events to Julia. "I'm sure he was looking for you. I could see the disappointment in his face when there was no one behind me."

Julia tucked her handkerchief in her dressing gown pocket. "Don't be silly. He was just doing a good deed. After all, the church was packed, and Papa was late."

"Well, after service, his first question was, 'Where's Miss Julia?'"

"Really?"

"Oh, yes, Julia. I'm so excited. It's so great to be in the middle of the—"

Julia was puzzled both by the event and her own reaction. "In the middle of what, Margaret? What are we into?"

"You should have seen him. When he saw father, he rose to his full height, bowed low, swept into the aisle, and invited Father, Mother, and me to pass in front of him to his pew. Even the minister stopped to pay attention. I do think the president was looking for you. You know, most of the time I feel—well—left out, second fiddle. But when the president is around, and you are belle, I don't mind at all."

"Really, Margaret, I think you are making more of it than you should. He probably wants Father to become ambassador—to England, I hope. I would love to be near Queen Victoria. She's so . . . well, regal."

Chapter 20
Romance Blossoms

Henry Wise visited John to discuss House issues. As he was about to leave, he turned to John. "This romance of yours is quite the talk of the town. Aren't you somewhat advanced in age to be involved in a lovescape?"

John grinned. "Nonsense, I'm in my prime!"

Wise seated himself again across from John. "There was a planter down on the James, not too far from your home. He decided to marry a younger woman. He was out in the field one day and he asked his old slave, Toby, what he thought. 'Massa, you think you can stand it?' The servant was incredulous. 'Why not?' the farmer asked. 'I'm yet strong. I can make her happy now as well as I ever could.' Toby replied, 'Massa, you is in your prime now, dat's true—but what about when she is in her prime? Where will your prime be?'"[vi]

John laughed, knowing the gentle gibe was well meant. But his determination was firm now. After his exchange with Wise, he decided to discuss the matter with no one. Letty and John Jr. were sullen in their silence. Robert and Priscilla did not encroach on his privacy.

It was a day when spring could be felt. The air was heavy with the scent of newly blossomed lilacs. The sun was warm on his back as he rode to Mrs. Peyton's. He was on his way to take Miss Julia and her sister to the King's Gallery, where a new collection was on display. *This is the day,* he thought. *This is the day when she will say yes.*

The gallery was poorly attended. They nearly had the place to themselves in the morning hour. Shortly after they started their tour, Margaret was attracted to a new display in an alcove. John swiftly moved Julia through the main hall in the opposite direction. His voice was low and intense. "You know that I do love you, don't you?" Julia looked away, and said nothing. "Possibly, I shall resign as president in order to devote my full energies to being once more a husband. That is, if the Honorable Judge McLean has not already won your affection in a permanent contract."

She turned to him. "No one has a permanent contract from me, Mr. President."

"But I'm seeking one. Will you marry me?"

Margaret entered the alcove behind Julia. Her cough startled Julia, who turned abruptly. John became aware that his suit was no longer a private matter. At this instant, it became a family affair. He was unsure of the consequences of this shift.

Julia darted an angry glance at the president. "I'm not ready for such commitment." She turned to Margaret and started to speak.

John stepped between the girls. "My feelings for you have not been secret, Julia. Certainly this does not come as a surprise to Margaret."

Julia's sigh was heart-wrenching for John. Surely he had displeased her. "We have not discussed it, Mr. President. Margaret cannot tell me how I feel if I don't know. But, now . . . please, take us home."

As the presidential carriage reached Mrs. Peyton's, the president got out in order to assist the girls. Colonel Sumpter and two other gentlemen were coming out the door. The president saw them, and they, him. His manner changed abruptly. Normally, he indulged in good-natured banter. Today, he assisted the girls and returned to his seat in haste. "Good day, Miss Julia, Miss Margaret."

As the horses plodded off, the girls looked at one another. Margaret opened her mouth, about to comment, but Colonel Sumpter interrupted. "Aha, Miss Gardiner, I trust you had an interesting adventure in the presidential coach." The colonel's eyes asked more than his words.

"We did, indeed." Julia said no more.

Margaret was grinning broadly. "Oh yes, sir."

After a pause, not so brief as to be embarrassing, the colonel asked, "Would you two lovely ladies care to join me on a visit to King's Gallery?"

Margaret started to decline. Julia curtsied just slightly, as was her custom. "We would be happy to."

"My pleasure. I will have the carriage here for you at about four o'clock."

When they were in the privacy of their room, Margaret asked, her voice irate, "Whatever are you doing?"

"Oh, there was enough at the gallery to make another visit pleasant, don't you agree, little sister?"

"You haven't answered my question."

"I'm keeping my options open. You saw the haste of the president's departure. Maybe he isn't ready to back up his offer."

"And you, are you ready to act on his words? I heard a proposal."

Julia furrowed her brow. "Not yet. But I'm not ready to turn him down, either."

***

John was still in mourning. God knows he missed Letitia, but when Julia was in the room, he felt twenty, even thirty years younger. He could not take his mind off her, nor when she was present, his eyes. Dismal as his political career was, solemn as the death of his wife had been, he knew that something important entered his life with the return of the Gardiners to Washington. One evening he visited Mrs. Peyton's when David invited him to join the evening whist game.

"Good evening, Miss Julia."

"Mr. President, so good of you to see us."

"The pleasure is all mine. You look . . . well, I'm speechless." All the while, he held her hand. Eventually she made a small gesture of withdrawal, and he appeared embarrassed but held on. "Miss Julia, it is difficult to part with even your fingers."

When the whist game began, John insisted Julia be his partner. "I do believe that Mr. Pickens and Judge McLean are jealous of me," said the president.

Julia blushed. "My sister can entertain them."

"How you feel about my intrusion is as important— no—more important than their feelings."

"Mr. President, I'm always pleased to be your partner. Ours is a winning combination."

"I do believe you are right, my dear."

"Oh! I didn't mean . . ."

He gently kissed her hand. "Oh yes, you did. You just don't know it yet. But I do."

***

On a bright, sunny morning, the president escorted the Gardiners home from church, his first public appearance with the Gardiner family. Until now he had only visited them, and they him, at home. When he returned home to the White House, John Jr. was angry.

"Father, you are making an ass of yourself!"

"Could it be, sir, that you are jealous? Let me remind you of many things, John. I loved your mother above life itself, and I still hold her memory dear. But I live and she does not. My life will continue. Furthermore, as you gallivant around town, you are not the eligible young man you wish you were. You, son, are a married man. I am not. I have years on you, but I am not in my grave yet. If Julia were interested in you, you would know it. She is not, I can assure you."

At a small gathering at the Executive Mansion, Julia was dressed in a white tarlatan, and on her head she wore a Greek cap with dangling tassel. When John saw her, she was dancing with Purser Waldron. At the end of the dance, the president claimed her for himself and took her to the library, where they were alone.

"I can contain my thoughts no longer, Miss Gardiner. Julia, my Julia, I want you to marry me."

"No, no, no!" John saw in Julia's eyes the look of a small animal cornered and threatened. Intimate as past conversations had been, he realized that just now he shocked her. He sensed her courage drain. At this moment, for the first time, John knew that Julia realized he was serious and talking about forever. What was to come of this request would shape their future.

Julia was silent, her eyes cast down. When she finally looked at John, she said quietly, "Please, sir, give me time to consider. Don't mention this to anyone." John touched her cheek gently. The seriousness of the moment circled them.

"I would not offend you for the world. You have such time as you need. But Julia, I do need you."

***

John Jr. grew increasingly difficult. He wrote Letty, his younger sister, complaining of their father's bizarre behavior. Her response was to make haste to Washington City. She had a sharp tongue, and was quick to scold her father after viewing an evening spent with the Gardiner family.

"Father." There was a particular timber that made this word a rebuke, shaming, harsh, and more like a parent to a child than child to parent. "You simply cannot continue in this manner. It does not befit your office, and it certainly does an injustice to our mother."

"You leave your mother out of this, young lady. I loved and still love her. But you must hear what John heard. She does not live. Mark that, Letty! She had my total affection while she was with me. I have her blessing to be myself now. You children have your lives. I have a term of office. I also have a life, and I intend to live it well and creatively. Now, I will hear no more from you about my suit."

***

Robert, behaving as if he were oblivious to all that was occurring around him, was a regular caller at Mrs. Peyton's. Invitations to the Executive Mansion were issued by him and accepted by David, all with a straight face, never alluding to the obvious.

"My father would be honored to see you and your family tomorrow night."

David was guarded. "The occasion?"

"Just an informal visit; Father mentioned that he lets go of the cares of State in congenial company."

David's eyebrow rose just slightly. "Tell your father that we will be honored to be present." David opened the mail and called to Julia. He showed her a letter that the *New York Post* carried. It was anonymous, but did indeed praise the president. "Do you know who wrote this, Julia?"

She read the clip and looked up. "No."

"Alexander did. I feel we are all doing our share."

Julia's brow furrowed. "Our share of what?"

"Our share of promotion . . . for success, everyone's."

"But I don't know . . ."

"You will, Julia. You will."

***

Julia's autograph book became the source of much difficulty that season. She loved to collect a few words from the rich and nearly famous. The season had added greatly to her supply of kind thoughts, placed in differing handwriting in the little book. Most of the boarders at Mrs. Peyton's made gracious additions and insertions. Near the end of the congressional session, Supreme Court Justice Baldwin signed it. He noted some missing names, and volunteered to carry the album to Capitol Hill to obtain significant signatures. Julia, pleased, consented.

In the book was a verse by Tyler, obviously intended for Julia alone.

> *Shall I again that Harp unstring,*
> *Which so long hath been a useless thing,*
> *Unheard in Lady's bower?*

Its notes were full wild and free,
When I, to one as fair as thee
Did sing in youth's brightest hours
Like to those raven tresses, gay
Which o'er thy ivory shoulders play
As stars, that through the veil of night,
Sent forth a brimy fire
I seize the harp, alas in vain
I try to wake those notes again
Which it breathed forth of yore
With youth its sound has died away
Old age touched it with decay;
It will be heard no more
Yet at my touch, that ancient lyre
Deigns one parting note respire.
Lady, it breathes of heaven.[vii]

David was angry when news of the poetry came back to him from the rumor mill. He called Julia into the family suite. "What in God's name were you thinking of?"

She stood in front of him, head down, contrite. Her voice was that of a small child. "I don't know. I didn't think."

"Julia, you are dealing with the president of the United States. You owe it to him and to yourself to think! This situation will cause him no end of embarrassment. He may even change his mind about you!"

"If he does, maybe it's a sign . . ."

"Of?" David's tone was icy.

Julia burst into tears and turned away. "I don't know." She ran upstairs.

***

The president's response when John Jr. burst into his study after hearing the news of the autograph book was undaunted. "Yes, I am writing poetry to her. I hope she will marry me, although she hasn't agreed yet. She hasn't said 'no,' either."

"Father, the family is using us. They want patronage. They want power. They will not hesitate to sacrifice the eldest daughter to get what they want. Don't count on her affection. You are an old man, and she is a child."

John jumped to his feet. "I may be old, but I recognize response when I see it."

"You recognize it when *you* feel it. You are experiencing your own response, Father. This affair isn't in your head. It's in your loins! And you are going to end up an old cuckold!"

"I forbid you to talk to me that way. Leave at once. You can be replaced!"

Chapter 21
Julia Receives a Formal Proposal

Julia was moody. She walked alone in the morning and avoided the family breakfast. She stayed in her room most of the day. David reminded her that the family was expected at the Executive Mansion for a small farewell dinner to end the season.

"I think I shall stay home. I have a headache."

David's voice was firm, bordering on irritation. "Nonsense, go rest. You will be fine by dinnertime."

"I don't want to go."

"Julia, we don't turn down invitations from heads of state."

"This isn't a state dinner, and I . . ." She ran from the room, crying.

"What was that all about?" David turned from the doorway to his younger daughter, who was sitting quietly by.

"She said she had a headache," Margaret echoed.

"Julia doesn't get headaches. She gives them. You follow her and tell her that she is going."

Margaret rose. Her slim figure was silhouetted in the afternoon sun coming through the window. "It isn't wise to force her, Papa. She needs some time."

"Time for what?"

Margaret hesitated. "Time to think. President Tyler is paying more attention to her than she can cope with."

"Go talk to her. Tell her I want her ready by seven o'clock."

Margaret left the room.

David's will prevailed, and Julia was persuaded to attend. It was an informal occasion. John Jr. was present, although he seemed sullen and uncommunicative. Letty was hostess. She greeted the family. "Mr. and Mrs. Gardiner and the children—hello, girls."

David said, "You know my daughters, Miss Julia and Miss Margaret?"

Letty minced her words, "Of course. They've been regular visitors here for a time, Mr. Gardiner. I'm sure everyone knows them."

Just then, Alice, John's youngest daughter, and Taz, his nine-year-old son, came into the drawing room. Letty said, "Let's go into the dining room. Father will be along shortly." Alice was guileless. Letty led the way, her lips pursed tightly. Her posture was rigid.

Taz's voice carried, "Miss Julia, you live in New York, don't you?"

"Yes. We live on Long Island. Do you know where that is?"

"Oh, yes. I studied it in geography."

He slid into a chair by Julia as she asked, "What else do you study?"

He paused and thought. "I've mostly learned to read, so now I can begin rhetoric and history. I like mathematics too."

Conversation was cut off as John offered grace. The four Gardiners were the only guests. Elizabeth and her husband, William Waller, were present. Over dinner, the president and David discussed the current political scene. David asked, "Will this new Republican party affect you?"

"I certainly hope not. They're largely anti-everything. I'd like to think even my opponents could do better than that."

David was thoughtful. "These are strange times. People whose parents were immigrants are suddenly opposed to our accepting aliens on our shores. People who left the old country in the name of free worship now want to limit others' rights to worship."

"These are indeed strange times," John agreed.

Julia whispered to Taz, "Will you take up politics too?"

The boy straightened in his chair. "I certainly hope not. I don't like what is happening to Father."

"But aren't you impressed with the good he is doing?"

"I wish Mr. Clay didn't undo everything and make Papa so unhappy."

Julia looked down at the young boy, who was suddenly intent upon finishing his meal. She turned her attention to the general conversation.

***

Later, upstairs in the family sitting room, John attended to the needs of his guests and then suggested that he had a new piece of music for Julia to try on her guitar. "Come with me. I think the music is in the downstairs library. You can become familiar with it before you face your fans."

The two left the room together. Letty snorted audibly. John Jr. poured generous after-dinner drinks. Margaret asked Alice if she did embroidery. Letty stood with her back to the guests. Taz's eyes followed the couple as they left the room.

John led Julia out of the room and downstairs to the library. Softly, he closed the door and said, "It would be possible to be married before next winter's social season, you know. You would be hostess here in the Executive Mansion, by my side. The place needs you. I need you, Julia."

"I don't know, John." She hesitated at the use of his first name. She thought of him as "Mr. President." Confusion and pain were evident in her voice. "When Victoria ascended to the throne and married, I envied her. I even thought I would enjoy the same kind of life, but now I don't know. I don't know what I feel. I don't know if it's you I love, or power, excitement, or the Executive Mansion and all that it stands for. John, you are talking about an entire lifetime—mine, yours, Taz's, Alice's, Letty's, all your children . . . I must know what it is I want before I agree."

"But you will agree, Julia, you will." He kissed her lightly on the forehead. Then he moved toward the door. Julia hesitated.

"Please, I need time."

He put his arms around her again. "I need you, Julia." He gently turned her face to his own and kissed her. Julia did not resist.

***

Once the Gardiner family was at home on Long Island, even though Julia had not accepted John's offer, a presidential wedding became a family issue. David spoke as if he wanted the issue settled the sooner, the better. He and Juliana were not in perfect agreement.

"Of course she will marry him!"

This conversation took place after dinner with the couple at the table, enjoying coffee. The girls returned to their rooms.

"Really, David, I don't see how he can care for her after he retires. He is noted to be impecunious."

"My dear, his family has never gone without a meal. He has property in Virginia, and he will always have power as an ex-president. She will be fine in his care. Julia has always been more comfortable with older men. Why should a marriage be any different?" For a few minutes only the sound of china cups being replaced on saucers was heard.

Juliana asked, "And what about that age difference?"

"Julia will decide that. You know as well as I do that our daughter will not be persuaded against her better judgment. But . . ."

"You do want to see them married, don't you?"

David avoided looking at Juliana. "That decision remains for Julia."

Upstairs, the conversation turned on a different point. Julia was lying across the bed, facedown. Margaret, waltzing around the room, turned to Julia and said, "He's in love with you. He really is." Julia could hear in her expression that whatever jealousy there might have been, Margaret was now a willing participant in her sister's romantic adventures. "Just think, I would become Robert's aunt! And an old maid aunty, at that! I think Henry Wise is an old dear, and Caleb Cushing, well he looks fine, but he cares only for you. And Mr. Pickens, well, I don't want to start out with four children. Even Colonel Sumpter—but all of them see you, not me."

Julia sat up. "I think John's attention just makes it a game with the others. Next season you will shine—if I decide to commit."

"Oh, Julia, are you going to?" Margaret jumped up to hug her big sister.

"I don't know. I really don't. I keep thinking about John and marriage and everything. There are no answers." Julia accepted her sister's embrace.

Chapter 22

Tension Increases

At the Executive Mansion, there was no easing of tension. Letty never missed an opportunity to chide her father. "You are behaving like a silly ninny. I'm so ashamed, I could die."

John Jr. joined her. "Really, Father, act your age."

John was as determined not to fight about his intentions as he was not to compromise. He guessed that his son might have personal motives for opposing the proposed union with Julia. He addressed his son in a straightforward manner, "I want Julia to marry me. I think she will. And I feel your mother would approve. In her last hours she told me that she wanted me to be happy after she was gone. Certainly, she had no reason to think I would join a monastery."

"Father!" Letty was horrified.

"Your mother knew me. She knew that I gave her all my love while she lived. She isn't living anymore, but I continue in my capacity to love."

"But a silly schoolgirl?"

John Jr. added, "And a hopeless flirt, younger than your own daughters."

"Julia is not silly. She is not a schoolgirl, and she may flirt with others, but I know her."

"What do you know, Father?" Letty's voice had a razor-sharp edge.

"I know she is wise and wonderful and honest and fair and . . ." His voice trailed off.

John Jr. spoke in icy tones, "Father, that's not your head talking. That's your loins."

John's face was red with anger. "Young man . . . I've warned you . . ."

***

At home in New York, Julia heard regularly from John. She read the unabashed love letters to the family, sharing them as if her life were a matter of family counsel. However, when the postmistress intervened, Julia was offended.

Margaret returned from her daily trip to the village and said, "Postmistress Stuart is aware that you've received letters more than once a week from the president. She wants to know if his intentions are honorable."

"Really, Margaret, and what did you tell her? It's mine that are in question."

"I didn't know quite what to say. She does see the letters coming in, even if she doesn't know the exact content. She knows you aren't working on a treaty with England."

On a brief visit home, Alex described the rumor mill in New York City. "People are saying that you have accepted his proposal only on the condition that he wins the 1844 election. You will campaign in Saratoga, I in the city with Tammany Hall. Other Tyler allies will take on the South."

"And if he loses, is it rumored I will abandon him?"

Alex smiled. "Well, it is rumored that Father and I will abandon him. If you are only engaged, you could break it off with no harm."

"You sound as if you approve of this arrangement."

"It's only what people are saying."

Julia's mind and heart were in Washington, however a family retreat to Saratoga came before any hope of a return to Washington for the season.

Late summer in New York State was cool, sunny, and pleasant. There were fancy dress balls and games of whist and tenpins. A passel of attentive young men became part of the package. David and Juliana agreed the excursion would be good for Julia.

Julia, the graceful and now of-age young woman, seemed to prevail. She was quiet; more reserved than she had ever been. She was also growing in grace. David watched his eldest daughter as they sat on the veranda. While he wondered what she was thinking, he knew his place was to wait to be invited to discuss the issue that preoccupied the entire family. Late summer in upstate New York was cool, at its colorful best. Father and daughter were sitting in companionable silence, watching a croquet game on the lawn.

Julia turned from the game and looked at her father. "You'd like it if I'd simply say 'yes' to the president, wouldn't you?"

"Julia, it is your happiness we are now talking about. I will not make that decision. The president of the United States has asked you to marry him. But we are not the crowns of

Europe, making decisions for our children based on geography and power. We are contemporary Americans. You have your future and your happiness to consider."

"But you do like him, don't you, Father?"

"Yes, I do."

"Do you think he will be a good husband?"

"He has a reputation for being one, but that offers a problem. Will you be happy with a man that much older than yourself?"

"Sometimes, when we are in public, he feels like you—like a father to me. But when we are alone and he looks at me, I know he is not my father and could well be my lover."

"Julia, you are young. You have many years of—" David stopped. He did not have the words to express his thoughts. "—development."

Julia seemed not to miss the implication. She looked at her father squarely. "Love? Yes, but it's not burned out in him. I just know it."

"But ten years from now?" David asked.

"Oh, who knows how I will feel ten years from now."

***

Juliana's thoughts on the matter of a presidential marriage were practical. "You'd better think how you will do in a farmhouse in Virginia, my dear. He might not win next year's election. He's not popular now, you know. Don't shut yourself off from the future. He isn't noted for his wealth and you, my pet, are a spoiled child. You have everything."

"I have money of my own."

"Not the kind you cost your father, you don't."

Julia wanted to return to the topic closest to her heart. "Sometimes I think I love him, and sometimes . . ."

"Is pleasing your father an issue?" Juliana moved across the room to be nearer to her daughter.

"He wants me to marry John, doesn't he?"

"It's because he thinks you will be happy, dear."

"But is that really his reason?"

"Your interests have always been uppermost with your father. It could not now be less. But I do believe his motives are mixed, more so than even he thinks."

***

The press issued regular releases on the political events of the day. Julia came to treat the daily news as her possession. David explained to her the intricacies of a third-party movement. "The president turned down an offer for third-party support in 1842 in Congress. He wanted moderates to support him then, especially since he faced such disdain within the Whig party."

"I remember that!" Julia thought back to her early adventures in the Hall of Congress. They seemed like such carefree adventures. Her main thought then was of the attention she could receive. What was actually happening on the floor was not at all for her to consider. Now, with John so real to her, the thought of the impeachment hearings sent a chill down her back. "Could he win in '44?" she asked.

"The *Aurora* is a pro-Tyler newspaper," David explained. "Alexander sometimes contributes to it. It says Tyler has support in Ohio, Virginia, New Hampshire, Virginia, and Pennsylvania, and there are Alex's friends at Tammany Hall. If these people can be pulled together, he may be able to create a party that can maintain control of Congress."

"But could he win an election?"

David folded the newspaper. "Being realistic, no, I don't think he could. Does that make a difference to you?"

Julia burst into tears and ran from the room. "I don't know! I don't know."

David turned to Juliana, but she spoke first. "Give her time, dear. You are asking a lot from her."

***

In New York, the social season was upon everyone. A flurry of shopping and a surge of favorable publicity for the president combined to dominate the Gardiner activity and conversation. Alex ran between the city and Washington with great delight, full of energy and certain that the world would be better for his work.

Upon return to Washington City the family, without Juliana, again settled at Mrs. Peyton's. They were quickly advised of the abundance of social activity.

At the White House, John headed the formal receiving line on a wintery evening. He was aware the moment the Gardiners entered the room. Purser Waldron and Judge

McLean escorted Julia and Margaret to the levee. David headed the group. Public affairs at the Executive Mansion were now infrequent but resuming. Much to John's disappointment, the group stood apart from the formal receiving line. John felt unable to break away from his social duties. He wanted some time with Julia. Priscilla, as hostess, was gracious and sociable, but John felt strangely incomplete and alone. In a brief, quiet moment, she leaned over to John and said, "Father, you seem ill at ease. That's not like you. Can I do anything to ease your tension?"

John had an almost boyish look about him. "I'd rather be elsewhere, my dear."

Just then a reporter approached him. "Mr. President, congratulations on this soiree. You are gaining in your popularity with the public by hosting such parties and opening the Executive Mansion to the public."

"To whom it belongs, sir." John did not mean to sound curt, although he considered the young man brash. He thought for a moment and added, "I am proud of the innovation. I believe an open affair at the White House ameliorates society. It is a Virginia notion, you know. It brings all classes of people together. We must Americanize socially as well as politically if we are to escape the evil distinctions and false notions of the European monarchies. Their notions of superiority will yield to our ideas of equality, if we are to give the proper illustration of our free institutions." He hoped that he would be favorably quoted in the press.

Julia saw him break away from the group around him as the last guest was acknowledged. She watched his graceful movement. The steps were effortless and light, as if he were dancing. He approached and greeted the family. He shook hands with the justice and lightly kissed both girls. Having taken Julia's hand, he did not let go. She could feel his pulse. He spoke, looking directly at her, "You and your family will be with me tomorrow on the excursion, I trust?" He seemed oblivious to the fact that they were part of a very public affair to which he was host.

"We are looking forward to it, Mr. President. Why is the event so special to you?" She enjoyed his attention. Her eyes locked with his. She felt herself reaching upward.

"You will be there." He smiled at her. She could feel his magnetism. He continued, "The USS *Princeton* is a new ship. It has come to us, and is the absolute pride of my former secretary of the navy, now secretary of state. You see, it is a family affair. But the real center of attention is the 'Peacemaker.' It's now the world's largest gun. We plan to fire it tomorrow. The shot will be heard all around the world. It will bring peace. I want it to be a day to remember for the American people. And, with you at my side, it will be a day for us also."

Julia dropped slightly in her curtsy and tipped her head. "We will be there, Mr. President, and it will, indeed, be a day we will remember." She felt as if a weight had been removed. As of that moment she had no doubt about her future.

As the guests started to leave, John invited select people to join the family upstairs for a cup of coffee. As the crowd dwindled and the select group headed upstairs to the family quarters, he took Julia's hand and hurriedly led her into the hall and downstairs.

She was nearly running and laughing. She pulled his hand to stop as they entered the pipe-laden, darkened hall of the lower floor. "Where are you taking me, John?"

"Come along, my sweet. The others can take care of themselves. Priscilla will make them comfortable upstairs. I want you to learn to play billiards."

They walked down the hall together now. John's arm was around Julia's shoulders, guiding and protecting her.

"Isn't it a man's game—all odds and positions, angles— not at all details that concern women?"

"On the contrary, it's like the game of life. It's risk. What if . . . it's how I look at life. Come on, let me show you." They entered the darkened room. John lit the lamps. It seemed as if the room sprung into being. "I've found this relic from Adams's time, here in the dungeon."

He watched as Julia looked around, noting eerie shadows in the corner cast by lamplight. The silence weighed heavily. John's heart was racing. He guided her to the table. His desire, mixed with a need for her commitment, possessed him.

Julia moved from him to the wall. She picked up a cue and turned back to the table. "So, you use one of these to hit one of those?" She pointed the cue to the balls, sitting in their triangular nest.

John picked up a cue and broke out the balls. "Here's how you hold the cue." He moved behind her and reached one hand to each of hers, pulling her arms forward while encircling her. He kissed her lightly. She did not resist. He guided her hand to place the cue on the table, and gently turned her around. Again, Julia, laying down the cue, offered no resistance. Instead, she reached up to embrace him freely.

Julia, at first winsome and flirtatious, suddenly felt a rush of desire that she didn't recognize. She wanted John's kiss, his touch. She was a willing, even eager participant as he kissed her.

"Marry me, Julia. Be mine."

She was flooded with a peace and joy she had never in her life felt. She was stunned by her own need, but said nothing. He kissed her again and gently disengaged from her. "We'd better return upstairs, or we never will."

Julia clung to him. "I . . . time, please, John, give me time."

"A lifetime, my sweet, is what I'm offering you."

Chapter 23

The "Peacemaker"

The following morning was cool but sunny. David, Julia, and Margaret were already aboard the USS *Princeton* and looking at the "Peacemaker," the new behemoth that held the hopes of its name, as the president arrived to board. From below, he spotted Julia at once and blew her a kiss. She gingerly waved back and turned to her father. Before she could say anything, Margaret was full of enthusiasm and news. "There's Will Waller! I wonder where Elizabeth is. Do you see John or Robert?"

Dolley Madison, wearing a gold lamé redingote, was standing with the Gardiners. She said, "Haven't you heard? Young John no longer works for his father. I think he left town. I don't know where Robert is. I can't imagine Priscilla missing this. Oh, look! The president is coming over to you, my dear!"

Julia was conscious that the charismatic gentleman wending his way toward her was concentrating on his mission, even as his admirers attempted to distract him with matters of state. She felt strange, almost giddy. He approached with a brief but cordial greeting and offered her his arm. "Miss Julia, will you join me?"

"My pleasure." She felt as if she were in a dream, on a stage, play-acting. As she tucked her gloved hand in the crook of his arm, she looked up. His smile was radiant, warming her in spite of the chill February air. She pulled her pelisse closer. It seemed the crowd moved back to make a path for the couple.

John and Julia led the tour. The gun was the center of attention. Its name embodied its intended use. It was a symbol to the world. John exuded joy. He leaned over and whispered, "I feel you are very close to saying yes."

She looked up and his glow was reflected in her expression. "I've been giving it careful consideration, sir." She dropped her eyes. "We have a lot to discuss." Then she returned her full gaze and added, "This is neither the time nor the place."

"We will find the place and make the time soon, my dear. I'm eager to begin a new life with you at my side. I want to talk to you about the coming election and the plantation. Oh, so much to say!"

Other guests approached and John was called away. Julia sought her father, who was deep in a discussion with Henry Wise and Abel Upshur.

". . . A third-party is his only chance. The Whigs won't have him. Henry Clay has never forgiven him."

"Nor he, Henry," Upshur interjected.

David continued. "And the Democrats are not ready to mend fences. Still, he has friends on both sides of the aisle. A third-party is definitely possible, especially if my son,

Alexander, is accurate in the picture he paints of the laborers in New York."

Upshur said, "John isn't that anxious to serve another term, but the annexation of Texas has become his dearest dream." He looked briefly at David, turned red, and mumbled, "One of his dearest dreams."

Wise continued, "Although, if he were to have a magnificent young lady at his side, another term would be desirable. Some men succumb to the sweet flavor of power, but power and romance combined are totally irresistible."

David returned the conversation to the election. "While he has many friends, they are neither Whig nor Democrat with enough consistency to win either nomination. At the time of mid-term election, he lost some support in Congress; you," he nodded toward Wise and Cushing. "But he did gain new allies. And his vetoes have not been overridden. Henry Clay's wings are being clipped by his own ego, and John is using power well. Maybe the Democrats . . ." his voice trailed.

"Not on your life." Upshur's round face was turned up to David's. "If Clay's unhappy with him, Jackson hasn't forgiven any Whig. And Jackson is still a major factor among the Democrats."

"If he could secure Texas . . ." David did not finish the thought.

Upshur said, "That may well be possible, but I fear it is not enough to secure the nomination."

"No, but a treaty annexing Texas could be very valuable. And it's possible."

"Possible!" Upshur's elf-like grin said more than his reply.

At exactly one o'clock, the *Princeton* weighed anchor and headed for Mount Vernon. The "Peacemaker" was fired twice. The cheers of an enthusiastic crowd were nearly drowned out by the noisy blast that actually shook the now-moving vessel. Guests gathered around the huge gun and listened as the captain described the novelty of the great new weapon. The guests treated the gun as if it were a huge, friendly watchdog that could be fierce if attacked but was a cozy homebody around the fire with friends.

Julia had been standing by her father silently. Abel Upshur spoke to David and Julia both. "Miss Julia, you seem to be official hostess today."

David's possessive smile demonstrated his pride as he responded, "Hardly, although I'm highly prejudiced on the subject. I feel she is definitely up to the job."

Julia nodded in acknowledgement and tugged on his arm. "Father, please, I'd like to talk to you."

David turned to his companions. "Well, gentlemen, I doubt any of you could resist such an invitation. Come, Julia, we will see what is happening below deck."

Julia could feel David's impatience as the two of them moved inward, beyond the crowd. She looked around. "I need to speak to you in private, Papa." They moved to clear a corner in the huge space. "Papa, last night . . ."

David waited until it was clear that she did not care to finish her statement. "Yes, Julia, go on. What happened last night?"

"That's it! I don't know what happened. I changed."

"And?"

"That's what I don't know. You would like for me to accept John's proposal, wouldn't you?"

David straightened his tie. "Your mother and I have discussed this matter at length. I want your happiness, Julia, just as she does. You yourself certainly show signs of wanting to marry him."

"Sometimes, I think I do, and sometimes I wonder if I'm simply being taken in by the glamour of the situation. The White House, an older man . . . you know, all the things around him. I don't know my own mind."

"But what about last night?" David carefully controlled his voice.

"Well, John took me downstairs to show me the billiard table that Adams left. And . . ."

"Yes?"

"Well, he kissed me."

"And?"

"I don't know. I wanted him to, and more . . ."

"Julia . . ." David's displeasure at the turn of the conversation was obvious.

"Well, Papa, I have to talk to someone about this!"

"Your mother is the appropriate person."

"But she's not here." They were at the ship's rail now. Both looked over the edge at the green water rushing by.

David softened. "You're right. I'm the only parent near, and you are my responsibility." After a brief reflection, he said, "Only you can decide if you love him and want to marry him. Only you can work between the glamour of the position as First Lady and the knowledge that a lifetime commitment is being asked of you."

"Last night, I wanted to marry him . . . now. I was ready to commit my life to him at once."

"And today?"

Julia allowed the question to hang in the air. "I'm contented to be by him. The hostessing is no problem. You and mother have given me good background for the amenities. So all I have to do is commit . . ."

"And?"

"I don't know . . ."

David allowed a pause. "Do you remember your thrill at court?"

Julia's memories returned to Paris, just a few years ago. The Gardiners were in a large drawing room in Paris with people like themselves, elegantly garbed, waiting in nervous anticipation for the royal couple to appear so the festivities could begin.

"Oh, Papa, I remember. I can hear the trumpets now and see the king."

"The queen followed. She wanted to make an entrance alone." David smiled at his daughter's sudden change in attitude. "She certainly managed to capture the attention of the crowd."

Julia looked at the moving waters. Her face glowed. "Red velvet and diamonds, yes, she did!" She turned to her father. "We could barely see. Margaret thought King Louis Philippe was a hundred years old."

"He may well have been, you know."

"But he was regal. His manner just fit the moment. He greeted us as Americans. I remember."

"And you, young lady, very appropriately answered in French. And then you promptly gave him a dissertation on American democracy, if you remember."

"He suggested I belong at court."

"And was he far from wrong?"

Julia looked up at her father's serious face. "You mean here? Now?"

"I'm asking, Julia. I sense that you must come to terms with John's suit soon."

"In some way, last night may have summed up my whole life."

***

Just after three o'clock, the ship changed course to return to Washington City. Julia was on deck with Margaret, David, and Purser Waldron, who was explaining the naval environment. William Waller approached them and spoke to Julia. "The president wishes to escort you into the collation which is just being served. I suppose you will have to obey orders."

"He is the commander in chief of the armed forces, and we are aboard a navy vessel." She turned to David. "You come, too, Papa." She seemed in high good humor, and she was aware that no one could eat until the president was seated. He would not sit until she arrived to be seated at his side. A warm glow filled her at the thought of John's possessiveness. *Would every day be like this one?* She found herself enjoying the feeling of belonging to John.

David kissed his daughter lightly on the forehead. "I'll be along. Go to your man. I want to find Upshur and Gilmer and be sure the Cabinet is behaving. Gilmer should know he has a good man here." He gestured toward Bursar Waldron, who saluted.

Although the area was normally used for storage, on this day it was converted into a dining room. Tempting platters of spiced blue crab, ham, fresh bread, and fruit, as well as elaborate pastries, filled the tables. Waiters carrying bottles of champagne filled the tinkling crystal containers held by passengers.

The president seated Julia at his right hand. He handed her a glass of champagne. Toasts flowed as generously as the libation itself. "Here's to the finest navy in the world, and to the finest ship belonging to that navy, and to her captain."

There were cheers. Other toasts followed, including one to the commander of the navy. Amid these amenities, John leaned over and whispered to Julia, "We could be toasting an engagement, if you were to consent."

"And we could be toasting Dolley Madison's one hundredth birthday, if she were a hundred."

"Must I wait until Dolley is a hundred?"

"That's not as long as it seems."

At the table a voice rose, suggesting that Captain Stockton fire the gun one more time in honor of George Washington, whose estate the ship was now passing. Stockton, proud host, was agreeable. He rose and suggested those who wanted should follow him. He would prepare another round.

The president rose to follow. Julia remained sitting. For a moment, she was alone. Instantaneously, an incredible melancholy descended upon her. She was swamped in a grief she could not understand. She wanted her father there beside her. She wanted to call to him as she had when she was a small child. She was distracted. Will Waller started singing, and the president returned to her side, laid his hand on her shoulder, and bade her listen to his son-in-law. John's presence steadied her. Normalcy returned. Everyone was silent as Waller ended his serenade, "Eight hundred men lay slain . . ." the conclusion of the war ballad.

"The Peacemaker" fired once more. The blast shook the ship violently. Waller's song seemed so right. A cheer went up from the delighted guests in the room. Before the cheers died, blood-curdling screams were heard from the deck. There was the clatter of frantic descent to the lower deck where the party was cheering. A ragged and sooty sailor entered the parlor. A trail of smoke and acidic odor followed him.

"A doctor! Is there a doctor?"

The president tensed. "Sir, come here and explain, please!"

"'The Peacemaker,' Mr. President, it ain't no peacemaker at all! Please . . ." The man broke into sobs.

John turned to Julia. "I must go, my love. Wait here."

"Father, my father! Papa . . ." Julia was in a panic and would not be left behind knowing her father was at risk.

John went above first, but Julia was right behind him. As he reached the deck, he turned to prevent Julia's following. It was too late. She was beside him. Jagged pieces of iron, some still red with heat, were everywhere. The smoke and smell made breathing difficult.

"The secretary of state is dead," someone announced.

John was still near enough that Julia felt him go rigid. Abel Upshur was a good friend and ally. She reached out to touch John.

"Stay here, Julia. I must see about Abel and the others, who . . ."

Upshur's body was one of how many? Julia moved to where she could see. The shipman tried to stop her, to protect her from the view of carnage. As he restrained her, she shouted, "I must find my father!"

John was sickened by what he saw, but he had to identify the dead and wounded. Abel Upshur and Thomas Gilmer were identified as among the dead. Virgil Maxy, who was a former charge d'affaires at The Hague, Commodore Beverly Kennon, Tyler's personal body servant, and two seamen were quickly identified among the fatalities. Among the wounded were the captain, Senator Thomas Hart Benton, and nine seamen. But the sight that cut to John's heart was the body of David Gardiner, the man whom he hoped to know as father-in-law. David was dead. John knelt near him. A seaman who was on deck at the time of the explosion knelt beside him.

"He went instantly, sir. I'm sure he felt nothing."

Although John was shaken, a terrible calm overtook him. "Julia, where is she? I must find her."

He retraced his steps to find her sobbing. "My dearest, do you want . . ." He could not finish his sentence.

"He's dead, isn't he?"

John put his arms around her shaking body. "I don't know the details, except that he died instantly, no pain. He never knew—"

"Take me to see . . ."

"Do you think . . .?" John felt her stiffen in resistance to his reluctance. "This way." Slowly, deliberately, he led her to the body of her father. She knelt, sobbing. John watched her body collapse in a faint. He gathered her motionless form and retraced his steps until he found Margaret, who was pale, standing woodenly. He told her what he knew, seated her, and laid Julia beside her.

A seaman approached him and saluted. "Sir, the *Johnston* is on its way. It will meet us and take the able-bodied back."

Margaret was feeling Julia's pulse. "Did she see Father?" John nodded. She remained statue-like in her quiet. "Do what you must, Mr. President. I will care for my sister."

John left the two girls, Julia still motionless. John was in an unbelieving daze as he sought Mrs. Upsure and Mrs. Gilmer, who remained below. He could not hear himself as he mouthed condolences to the women. The frail body of Julia lying against Margaret was etched in his brain.

As the *Johnston* made preparation to take on the wounded and bereaved, John returned to Julia. She started to rise, but her legs would not hold. He picked her up again and carried her to the gangplank of the other ship. Julia awakened, realizing that John was carrying her. She struggled to free herself. "Papa . . . I want to . . ."

"Calm, my love, you must be calm. I'm moving you to another ship for safety. I must return to the others."

"My father, is he . . .?"

"Yes, my darling. It was fatal for him and for others, too."

She started to sob. She could feel John's firm grip. It seemed that only his touch held her together. He carried her across the plank from one ship to the other. A naval officer followed with Margaret. Margaret was on her feet and seemed self-possessed. "I'll take care of her, Mr. President. You go to the others." Margaret sounded composed.

From somewhere in her darkened interior, Julia heard John say, "I will send a courier for your family as soon as we get back. Take Julia to your rooms, and wait until you hear from me. Someone will be with you. As soon as I've made contact with your mother, I'll come to you." Julia felt herself being placed on a deck chair. He kissed her hair and turned to go.

Julia was crying as Margaret put her arms around her sister. As Julia regained composure, Margaret's attention reminded her that both of them, after all, lost a father. She reached out. The two girls clung to each other as if they were the only survivors in a world of disaster. Indeed, for their world, it was so.

John returned to the grisly work aboard the *Princeton*. There, personal and political tragedy mixed in overwhelming proportions. John moved from body to body and made mental preparations for appropriate viewing at the Capitol. His grief encompassed the loss of trusted friends and advisors. And Julia's suffering was as his own. In the dim recesses of consciousness, he wondered if this would make a difference. He decided that Senator Gardiner should have the honors due his Cabinet, and proceeded to make preparations.

Chapter 24
The Aftermath of Tragedy

Dolley Madison immediately took charge of the Gardiner girls. She dispatched a messenger to the White House, telling John that Julia and Margaret were at her home. She was caring for them rather than burden either sister with the other. She wanted to console both girls. Would he contact the family? More immediately, he should see Julia.

Julia was on a guest bed at Dolley's. She was floating in and out of a fitful sleep. She seemed to hear John say, "I've sent a courier for your family. It will take time for him to get there, but I'm certain your mother will come as quickly as possible. I'll contact young David and Alexander, too." She felt herself crying as if she were a puppet. Margaret appeared composed. She sat on the bed near her sister, but not touching her. As Julia regained consciousness, she reached out to Margaret to give and take comfort.

***

After the ship docked, Henry Wise accompanied John back to the Executive Mansion. John noted the memo from Dolley. "I want to go to Julia."

Wise said, "Not yet. You must provide appropriate wakes for Upshur and Gilmer, contact the army, and make provisions for laying out at the Capitol. We need to recognize Maxey in some way, too."

John listened silently. He rose, faced Wise, and calmly stated, "David Gardiner will lie with them."

"John, are you mad? Those two are part of your Cabinet, your other thinking self. David Gardiner is nothing but a—"

John turned to him. His eyes were fiery. "David Gardiner would be my father-in-law if . . . He will have the honors of state."

"You can't!"

"Oh, yes, I can."

The president's son, John, entered. His condition demanded attention from the older men. "How is my father responding to tragedy?" The words were slurred. His gait was less than steady.

John became very formal. "Son, I could have used your assistance tonight. Go!"

"How was the wench today, Father?"

"What?" John turned to Wise. "Excuse me, Henry. I will take care of this problem at once. Then we can return to other matters."

"Oh, she was good. I always thought she would be."

Wise scurried from the room.

"You are being rude. Leave here at once."

"Did you find out last night? Or are there secret rooms aboard the ship?"

"What are you talking about?"

The young man pulled a necklace from his pocket. "I found this on the pool table. Where were you, Father?"

"John! Stop that. Nothing . . . not . . . that's not how it was. None of this is any of your business. Go pack your bags and go."

John Jr. was laughing now. "Ah, she *was* good! I always thought there was something bawdy about her body. Ha! I made a pun, while Dad . . ."

"Go! Now." The president's voice was edged in steel. "Get out!"

John Jr. stumbled to the door. He left. Henry moved slightly.

The president went to the window. He was breathing heavily. "I could have done without that!"

Henry was searching for soothing words. "I'm sure these must be trying times for the whole family. Your children suffered the loss of Letitia, and now this tragedy overlying everything else . . ."

John's voice was filled with a terrible calm. "Henry, if you are the friend you purport to be, prepare to have Upshur, Gilmer, and Gardiner lying in state at the Capitol two days hence. I will contact Mrs. Upshur, Mrs. Gilmer, and Mrs. Gardiner about burial and services. Now I must go to Julia, contact her mother, and do what I can there."

Henry started to interject.

"My mind is made up, Henry. He will have the recognition of state. No argument."

The little man pulled out his handkerchief and wiped his forehead. He shook his head, and said, "If you insist, but—"

"I insist."

***

At Dolley's, John was admitted to the library where the three ladies were huddled near the fire. As he entered, Dolley rose to greet him. "Mr. President, the doctor gave Julia and Margaret some sleeping medicine. As soon as we are certain Mrs. Gardiner has been contacted, I will give each of them a dose." John moved around the petite dynamo and over to the crumpled figures of the girls.

"Are you all right, Julia?" He knelt in front of her.

She looked at him. "I don't know. I hardly know what happened. I want Mama."

"We'll get her here as soon as possible. The courier has been contacted. He may be at your home with your mother." He started a personal note.

> *Dear Mrs. Gardiner, we regret to inform you there has been a tragic accident aboard the Princeton. Your daughters were unharmed, but Mr. David Gardiner . . .*

John stopped. How can this be said?

> *David was killed instantly upon the backfiring of guns on deck.*

He finished the note and left the room to find his servant.

When he returned he assured the girls that their mother would be near soon. He wanted to hold Julia, but something in her manner told him to keep a distance between them. He sat near the fire. "I'm making provisions for your father to lie in state at the Capitol with members of my Cabinet."

"Isn't that an honor reserved for—" Julia hesitated.

"I feel he was nearly a member of my family."

"Mr. President . . . John, I'm not . . . I don't know." Julia started to sob.

John put an arm around her gingerly. "Julia, we can sort everything out later. For now, accept that he was important to me." He could see fear, exhaustion, and grief weighing on Julia. "For now, Julia. Just for now." *You will have all the time you need to make a decision.*

***

Juliana was alone at home when the courier arrived. She opened the presidential note and fainted. The courier caught her. He and the maid moved her to the sofa. The maid then dispatched the courier to Alexander's office with the news. Within two days, David Lyon-Gardiner's second son Alexander, and Juliana arrived at Mrs. Peyton's to be with the two mourning girls. They had been attended by aides from the White House from the time they left Dolley's personal care.

Juliana drew her four children together. "We are alone. We must make the best of it. Your father left us secure in many ways."

"Mama, he's gone. How can you think of such things?" Julia was weeping.

"You children have much to learn about survival. It comes before mourning as well as after. I love your father. I always will. But right now, we must get on with life. Alex, you are the official head of the family."

He said, "Your example is important, Mother. I hope I can show the composure and courage you do."

"You will, son. All of you will. You are David's children." She turned to the window, concluding the conference.

***

The presidential carriage arrived to take the family to the Capitol where David lay in state with the other fallen leaders, so that a nation could mourn. The caskets were aligned Upshur, Gilmer, and David Gardiner. The family was escorted to the arrangement amid the solemn lines of mourners passing through. Julia had regained her poise, but the sight of her father's casket caused tears to well up again from a place so deep it seemed outside herself. She put her arms around her mother as the older woman started sobbing. Alexander caught them both in an embrace. David Lyon and Margaret stood apart, less demonstrative of pain.

The president entered the room, causing little stir from the mourners. He went directly to the Gardiner family. Taking Juliana aside, he said, "I've made arrangements for your husband's remains to be located until you are able to prepare for a suitable burial. I understand the suddenness of this."

"Thank you, Mr. President. My family is grateful."

"You know I feel very close to your family, don't you?"

"So I understand. But you realize the present circumstances preclude . . ." Juliana didn't finish the sentence. John bowed his head in understanding assent.

***

The funeral was held on Saturday morning, a single service for all three leaders. The day was cold and blustery. John's carriage headed a stately procession. The City of Washington was closed in memory of those who passed on. The president and all the military and diplomatic corps escorted the bodies to the Capitol where services were held for the three men.

John sat with Letty, his oldest daughter, John Jr., Robert, and Priscilla in the front row. Juliana and her family were in the second row. The Upshur and Gilmer families were across the aisle. As service concluded, the four families were the first to move to the Capitol steps with John, who spoke briefly to Julia. "My dear, if only I could be with you."

"You have so much now, John, dear; your Cabinet, your friends, and the whole nature of the tragedy. I should like to help you." No one, not even Julia, noticed the change of address.

He kissed her hand and moved on. He was drawn away from the Gardiner family now, in deference to his role as chief mourner at the wake of all three gentlemen. The others' families were no less in need of his presence and company. He did not, however, let the Gardiners out of his range of vision. John ached to be with them. His feeling of privation was dominated by the loss of David Gardiner, his ally in politics and, he was certain, in romance. David was a man whom he genuinely admired and whose advice he sought. But more than his feelings, David held the key to the young lady's heart. Now maybe all was lost. John's support from within Julia's family seemed gone. Juliana appeared calculating, much less amiable. John sensed this difference. Even though he had never discussed his romantic inclinations with David, there had been a subtle sense of approval. The family was full of unknowns, not the least of which were Julia's own feelings. And even if those were positive, the loss of her father would now make matters much more difficult.

As everyone prepared to move to the location for the burial of Upshur and Gilmore, John came over to the family. He took Julia's hand. His expression of love and concern for her once again confronted her. It was so deep she felt as if she'd fallen into the sea. She stood transfixed. Time stopped. He appeared so open and vulnerable. Julia experienced a feeling she did not recognize. He gently kissed each woman; Juliana, Margaret, and last, Julia. He held her face with a lingering, wistful gesture so gentle, and gazed at her for just a second, then moved on to his own carriage. Julia's eyes followed him. Even after the carriage door closed and the coachman prepared to move, he watched her.

***

Henry Wise was at his side. Quietly, as they rode in the carriage, Henry started to point out the vacancies in the Cabinet.

"Not now, man. Can't you let politics alone, even in the face of death?"

Henry wore his usual cherubic face, now solemn, as befitted the occasion. "Politics do not go into mourning, Mr. President."

"Nor do affairs of the heart!" John spoke to himself.

"Politics is a matter of the welfare of the country. By God, John, don't equate your Cabinet with that woman you're playing games with."

"I'm not playing games. I grieve the loss of all three of those men."

"I still can't believe you have Gardiner lying in state with your Cabinet members. It's an insult to public service."

"David served me well in ways you will never understand, Henry. He listened, sometimes without imposing his own views." John's intended rebuke seemed to take hold. Henry was quiet.

"You have many concerns: the loss of friends and the seamen. The families all look to you for comfort. You are, after

all, commander in chief . . . and your own manservant . . ."
Henry's genuine sympathy eased the tension.

"Fortunately, the body can only acknowledge so much
pain. After that, numbness allows me to do what I must."

At the cemetery, where Upshur and Gilmer were to be
interred, Julia watched John accept the sympathy of well-
wishers. Her own and the other families did the same. As
the crowd thinned, he approached the Gardiners. His
expression penetrated Julia so deeply she felt as if she were
wounded again by his pain. She stood, transfixed, for just a
moment. He was so open and vulnerable in that second,
that Julia experienced her love for him anew. He came over
and kissed each of the women, briefly held Julia's face with
a lingering wistful gesture. Then he moved toward his own
carriage.

Julia's continued to watch him, and she sensed that she
was in his sight as the separation continued. For all the
tragedy of the day, she was certain now of her feelings.

Something frightened the horses. Just as John's carriage
was pulling away to return to the city, they bucked and ran
off, causing his carriage to totter precariously. It came near
to toppling over. Julia watched in stark terror. As the
horses were brought under control, Julia began to shake
uncontrollably. She started to cry, not in hysteria, but in
deep mourning sobs. Her love for John Tyler and for her
father blended into one great ache. For an instant she knew
utter despair.

Chapter 25

John Regroups

With the Gardiners' return to New York to make plans for David's final resting place, John once again found it necessary to create a Cabinet of trustworthy men. At his door, intrigue was afoot. This time, a friend made a move that tested the term "friendship."

Henry Wise saw Senator George McDuffie from South Carolina by appointment. The conversation was most unexpected by McDuffie, who knew that Henry and the president were allies. He also knew that John was an ardent supporter of the Union. The president held most Southern representatives aloof, especially those who spoke openly of secession. Wise passed the time of day, expressed sorrow at the loss of so many good men, and finally made his move.

"Senator, would you have any access to the mind of your esteemed colleague from South Carolina, Senator Calhoun?"

"Oh come now, who can know the mind of that man? What are you thinking, sir?" McDuffie was unsuspecting.

Henry's words were measured. "I would presume to know if Senator Calhoun would have a mind to become secretary of state. Because if he would, his name could, in all probability, be sent to the Senate at once."

Except to blink, McDuffie controlled his reaction. Coming from Wise as this proposal did, it necessitated an urgency to act quickly. No doubt, President Tyler was its source. The moment Wise left the office, McDuffie sat down and penned a note to Calhoun with total assurance that, since the suggestion came from Wise, it had to be initiated by the president.

Wise left the meeting with McDuffie and went to the White House for a late breakfast with the president. He found John red-eyed, talking to Judge John Christian, his brother-in-law.

"I still can't believe what happened. I saw five bodies, three of my closest friends, and my personal body servant lying on the deck." He choked up again, and then continued as if an inner force were driving him to relive the scene.

Henry lingered through the morning with John. Eventually Henry, partly from his own need to confess, and partly to change the topic and turn the President's attention, calmly announced, "I offered state to Calhoun. Well, not exactly, but . . ."

"You what?"

"Well, I suggested to McDuffie that Calhoun could be secretary of state if . . ." There was deathly silence. "It was presumptive of me, I know. But John, we need your Texas position protected. Cal is the best man in the country to do that right now. He believes in expansion."

There was a long silence. John stared at nothing. When finally he spoke, his tone was unmistakable. "How could you do this to me?"

"It's in your best interest, John. Cal is what you need."

"I've always considered you a friend, but this is an act just short of treason." John rubbed his jaw as if he had been dealt a physical blow.

"John, you need—"

"Don't tell me what I need. He will politicize the issue hopelessly. He can't tell the difference between Texas, nullification, and slavery. All the things I want to keep separated, he lumps together. He brings nothing to the office of state. He neither understands nor cares about international concerns. I've stopped this suggestion twice, once when Daniel stayed and again when I appointed Upshur. Now you . . ."

"Of course, you could deny that the idea was yours, repudiate me . . ." Wise's voice trailed off.

John was yelling now, uncharacteristically. "You are the most extraordinary man I ever saw. The most willful, wayward, incorrigible . . .!"

Something in the diatribe clued Henry that the battle was won. "Nevertheless, you will accept Calhoun?"

"I have no earthly reason to! Let me think!"

***

It was a long and sleepless night for John. In the wake of the multi-tragedy, his closest friend had betrayed him in monumental fashion. John C. Calhoun was insane. He had no gifts to add the office of secretary of state. A diplomat he was not, at least not in these, his older years. His pro-slavery views and his nullification principle tainted every act, every word. Since taking office, John had been careful to separate his views on slavery, states' rights, and the need to see Texas as part of the Union. Calhoun's appointment would undermine this separation hopelessly.

At breakfast the following morning, he was alone and still in doubt concerning the wisdom of letting Wise's offer go unchallenged. He hurt over the necessity of denying his good friend publicly. Priscilla came into the dining room. "You have something on your mind, Father Tyler?"

John looked up. Julia, sadly, was nowhere near. She certainly would have been his comfort. However, this lovely and intelligent young lady might very well help him clarify his own thoughts. "Sit down, Priscilla. I want you to hear something."

She pulled a chair from across the table and sat facing John. He poured out the whole story.

"I have been diligent in separating the concept of annexation of Texas and the slavery issue. There are many Northerners who see the economic advantage of annexation. I see no reason to antagonize them. Antislavery advocates see Texas becoming not one, but many slave states. The Great Compromise allowed states' admission of one slave with one non-slave, thereby maintaining a precarious balance. If Texas were to presume an inner division, the Union could be in jeopardy."

"Where does Mr. Calhoun stand on the Texas issue, Father?"

"Everything he does translates into the protection of the states from the Union. But he does approve of annexation. The problem is alienation of people who want annexation, but abhor his nullification views, and fear his secessionist tendencies. Annexation would give us a virtual monopoly on cotton worldwide. We would hold the key to international economy with Texas as part of the Union, and an ocean-to-ocean country would be in sight. A pact with Texas to remain perpetually undivided would be advantageous."

"Do you think Calhoun will drive many away of those who otherwise agree on Texas?"

"Calhoun could drive his own mother away!"

Priscilla leaned forward. "Wait a minute. Think. Who would be affected on the Texas issue by Senator Calhoun's position in the Cabinet?"

John was silent for a thoughtful period. "I can put very few faces or names with that position . . ."

Priscilla seemed to relax. "Now, what are the other immediate problems Senator Calhoun would be addressing?"

"Well, there are the Brits and Texas. An Anglo-Texas treaty would bring Her Majesty to the borders of the States on two sides. They are already to the North. They would come very near to encircling us. The Asburton Treaty holds them up North, but if they were to get together with Mexico, Texas' independence would be undermined. We were negotiating directly with Texas. I want someone who will follow through."

"Will Calhoun?"

"He may. But we have forty-two votes in the Senate. I don't know what Cal can hold. And worse, the secrecy of negotiation is important. I have no confidence that Calhoun is capable of secret negotiation."

"But you don't know that he won't manage in secret, do you?"

"No, I just don't trust him to do anything as I ask."

Priscilla seemed to be leading him to a conclusion based on his own thinking. "What are the arguments for his appointment?"

"I have no good one, except that Henry has himself out on a limb. He made the offer in my name without consulting me. If I refuse to go along with it, I lose Wise supporters, Calhoun supporters, and lend fuel to the fire of all those who say I can get along with no one."

"I think you've descried your plight and its solution very well, Father. You've loaded the record in favor of his appointment in as far as I can tell."

"Have I?"

"Think about what you've just said."

To repudiate Calhoun now would alienate and embarrass Henry forever. Henry was his best friend and only confidant. It would also antagonize Calhoun's allies in Congress. John held a fragile group together. Not a majority, but enough to sustain a veto. They could be counted on occasionally with Henry's help, and he would need all of them when Texas came up for approval.

The next morning, he saw Wise. "Henry, what you have done is dastardly. My loyalty to you will jeopardize all that

I hold dear in this term of office. You have strained our relationship to the breaking point."

Henry heard the president through. He allowed the silence between them. Finally, he began, "Then you—"

John turned his back and said, "Take the office and tender it to Mr. Calhoun. You may want to write him yourself."

There was a meaningful moment of silence. Henry was subdued when he responded, "Thank you, Mr. President. I do believe you will not regret this decision."

"Just go!"

Chapter 26

Julia's Decision

In East Hampton, a family mourned the loss of its father. Julia matured in the face of tragedy. Julia dreamed of her father. She dreamed of John Tyler, president of the United States and her suitor. Sometimes the dreams blended until she could not distinguish between the men. She woke, knowing that she loved them both. One was gone forever. The other wanted an answer to a fervent request for marriage.

"Last night, I was all in white, except for the black stone on my head. I was in a big hall. Papa was there with me. He took me to the president and put my hand in John's."

Juliana listened to her daughter. She was quiet now, no advice to give. She recognized grief and affection. The family shared grief.

"Then, I was in water, drowning. Papa supported me, but someone reached over and tried to pull me out." Both Margaret and Juliana listened without comment. Neither quite knew how to direct her.

The correspondence from John was gentle but persistent. Julia read and reread his letters. She spent time alone. Her sleep continued to be filled with dreams that blended her father and John into one image. Finally, she indicated that she would prefer a marriage earlier than later.

John wrote to Juliana:

> *I have the permission of your daughter, Miss Julia Gardiner, to ask your approbation of my address to her, dear madam, and to obtain your consent to our marriage, which in all dutiful obedience she refers to your decision. May I indulge the hope that you will confer upon me the high privilege of substituting yourself in all that care and attention which you have so affectionately bestowed upon her. My position in society will, I trust, serve as a guarantee for the appearance which I have, that it will be the study of my life to advance her happiness by all and every means in my power.*

Juliana studied long and hard before she answered the president of the United States. He might have social standing, but her daughter was used to the best. Indeed, the Gardiner girls did not know anything else existed.

> *In reply to your letter received day before yesterday, I confess, I am at a loss what to answer in return. The subject is to my mind so momentous and serious, rendered doubly so by my own recent terrible bereavement, that I know of no considerations which this world could offer that would make me consent without hesitation and anxiety to a union so sacred, but which death can*

dissolve. The deep and solemn emotions of my mind are not to be regarded as criterion of the mind of others. Neither do I desire by any reference to my own feelings to cast a shade over the future hopes of those whose anticipations of life are comparatively unclouded. Your high political position, eminent public service, and above all unsullied private character command the highest respect of myself and family and lead me to acquiesce in what appears to be the impulse of my daughter's heart and dictates of her judgment. In cases of this kind, I think the utmost candor should prevail, and I hope you will not see the suggestions I consider my duty as a mother to urge other than wise and proper. Her comfortable settlement in life, a subject often disregarded in youth but thought of and felt in maturity, claims our mutual consideration. Julia, in her tastes and inclination, is neither extravagant nor unreasonable, tho' she has been accustomed to all the necessary comforts and elegancies of life. While she remains in the bosom of my family, they can be continued to her. I have no reason to suppose but you will have it in your power to extend to her the enjoyments by which she has been surrounded and my references to the subject arise from a desire to obviate all misunderstanding and future trials.[viii]

Thus, a reluctant consent was given. From the receipt of Juliana's letter, plans were made, carefully, for a June presidential wedding.

***

Alexander was ushered into the reception room at the Episcopal Offices of New York on Saturday, June 22. The summer sun shone through the window, creating a pattern of light and shadow that his eye followed as he waited. The bishop entered the room. Alex rose and introduced himself.

"I have a request of some import. I am the elder brother of Miss Julia Gardiner, who has recently become engaged to President John Tyler." Alex was trying to sound matter-of-fact, but the simplest explanation seemed to cause eyebrows to raise. Alex's heart beat rapidly.

Bishop Onderdonk gasped. "She is very young, isn't she?"

"She is mature, Your Excellency, and very conscious of her own mind. She and the president are deeply in love. If possible, we would like you to officiate. The ceremony is to be at the Church of the Ascension at two o'clock on Wednesday, June 26. Father Bedell, the rector, will be asked to assist you. He is our pastor."

The bishop consulted his date book. "It sounds possible. What about bans?"

Alex cleared his throat. "We hoped that you would give them a dispensation. You do understand the importance of absolute secrecy, don't you?" He wanted to keep the interview brief. Too many questions would expose his own doubts.

"I most certainly do. How large a party do you plan?"

"Our family is small. There are five of us now. I'm not sure whom the president will ask to witness. One or two additional families will complete the guest list. All of us are, of course, in mourning. My father, you know, passed away just four months ago. At the same time, members of the presidential staff did also. If the matter were to become public, it would become very public."

"Isn't he still in mourning over his wife?" The bishop's brow furrowed.

"She died some two years ago, and was ailing before that. She held a special place in his life that cannot be replaced, but he has been without her for some time."

"Indeed. Well . . ." He turned away to absorb the information, then faced Alex. "I must take your word on the wisdom of this union, but you have my word that I shall reveal it to no one. I'll cover my appointments book so that not even my wife will know where I'm to be."

Alexander returned home, content that his mission was well underway.[ix]

***

Julia couldn't make up her mind what to do about a dress. "I shouldn't wear white because of Papa's recent death, and I can't wear black. It's John's second marriage, but my first. He's barely out of mourning for his wife, and there are the other recent deaths. Maybe the whole wedding party should be in black! Oh, Mama, what'll I do?"

Juliana took command. "Of course you will wear white. Anything else would be a disservice to your father. He valued your virtue, and dearly desired your marriage to John."

"We could put her in violet, and let the tongues wag," Margaret said.

"Hush! It's difficult enough without your nasty remarks," Juliana said.

"He was my father, too." Margaret turned to the window to hide her tears.

Julia looked at her sister's back and, realizing Margaret's turmoil, went to her and put her arms about her little sister. "Margaret, I can't do this without you. I need you near me. I must know that you will be there for me when nobody else understands."

Juliana added, "Yes, and with Julia out of the way, you will have the pick of Washington's crop next season. Your extroverted sister will be a matron."

"And a hostess to end all hostessing!" Margaret's smile lightened the surroundings.

"Precisely, my dear." Julia determined that the crisis was over. "Now, about your dress, Margaret?"

"I think I shall wear a dark green voile. It will be as becoming as can be, and I can avoid looking like either a junior bridesmaid or your mother."

"There's nothing wrong with looking like her mother." Juliana's crisp words relieved the tension.

Julia chose a simple dress of white lace. A total absence of jewelry would be her concession to mourning. She would have a gauze veil descending from a circle of white flowers that lay on her brown curls. Her hair would be pulled back from her face, parted in the middle and pulled into buns over each ear, emphasizing her dark, expressive eyes.

Julia was radiant in spite of occasional lapses into a very real grief at the loss of her father. Her five-foot-three height, narrow waist, and full bosom established a beautiful form. Her natural enthusiasm, combined with the growing feeling for John, combined to give her a unique glow.

***

Upon return from shopping in Manhattan, Juliana and Julia sat down for tea. The conversation began with a review of the day's purchases and consultation with the list on what remained to be done before the wedding. Julia was silent for a moment, then turned to a new subject.

"You and Papa were in love, weren't you, Mother?"

"In love? Yes, I loved your father very much, and he, me."

Julia hesitated. "Were you happy? Did you like . . . it?"

Juliana studied her daughter, as if to be certain she had received the correct message in the question. "Intimacy?"

"Well, yes. Oh, Mama, I can hardly wait. I wonder . . ."

Juliana was quiet. The world around them did not allow for expression of these thoughts among the genteel. But Juliana was confronted with Julia's openness. Proper instruction was terribly important. Juliana felt she had neither the experience nor the vocabulary to prolong this conversation. She reminisced briefly, and then ventured, "If you love him, you will like it. If you don't, you won't."

"Oh, Mama, I know I will!"

"You know that marrying an older man will . . . well, make a difference, don't you?"

Julia was surprised. "It will? How?"

"Goodness, child, I can't tell you anything to begin with, so how can I tell you what is different? Except . . . well, as people age, intimacy may become less important."

"Oh, I hope not!"

"Really, Julia!" Although Juliana's tone was scolding, her attitude was one of pleased embarrassment.

Chapter 27

The Wedding

The gloom and grief that surrounded John since the tragedy was lifted. His loneliness was at an end. Although the actual date was not to be mentioned to anyone, John told his friend and confidant Henry Wise. Henry was astounded that John had won the love-match lottery from the prior season. "And she's agreed to marry . . . you?"

"Yes, and why not?"

"You are far too advanced in life to be imprudent."

"How do you mean imprudent?"

"Easy, you are not only past middle age, but you are president of the States, and that is a dazzling dignity which may charm a damsel more than the man who holds the office."

"I know my woman, Henry. I'll be fine."

***

Alice, John Jr., and Letty were together in the family quarters. When John entered, the quiet made it clear that there had been a family conference. The topic might be easily guessed.

"Children, Miss Gardner has accepted my proposal. We are to be married, though I cannot say how soon." The silence was ominous. "Your congratulations and good wishes are in order."

John Jr. was the first to speak. "You are making a damned fool of yourself."

"Son, I'll hear none of that. Is it just possible you are jealous?"

"Nonsense, she's . . . well, she is not my type." He turned from his father.

"Possibly you should spend more time endearing yourself to the wife you have, and less trying to discourage me."

Letty was no more satisfied with her father's decision. "The press is already having a field day. Now, you hope to legitimatize their remarks?"

"Do not speak of my relationship to Julia, and certainly not my marriage, in that fashion. I plan to complete my life. Marriage is a state that becomes me. I enjoyed life with your mother. In her absence, I realize my needs. Julia fulfills those. And I'm led to believe that I fill a place in Julia's life."

Alice was the last to break her silence. Her tone was not querulous, just curious. "Will someone not much older than me really make you happy, Father?"

"Julia will make me happy. I am certain of that. And I think that, if you give her an opportunity, she will add immeasurably to your lives also."

"Humph, not to mine." Letty was sullen. She rose and walked to the window, turning her back to her father.

John studied each of the three children. "She will make no pretense as to her relationship with you. She is not your mother. But she is a wise and imaginative lady who can prove to be a very good friend, if you allow her."

John Jr. stood and turned his back to John, who hoped the silence was a healing one; the beginning of acceptance. Only Letty continued in her original mode. "Nonsense, disgrace, desecration to my mother, and to the office of the president . . ."

***

The Gardiners had no guest list. They decided that only the immediate family would be present. John very specifically and carefully requested that John Jr. be with him. Other than family, he invited Postmaster General Charles Wycliffe and his wife and daughters, Mary and Nannie. Caroline Legare, daughter of the late attorney general, and Colonel and Mrs. John Lorimer Graham completed the list of wedding guests. Alexander was to be groomsman.

On Wednesday, June 26, at noon, the ceremony was performed. On Alex's arm, Julia moved up the aisle of the church. She was aware of the guests clustered in the front of the church. Julia felt an all-encompassing calm, as if not she, but a greater force was moving her body.

In front of the alter, John waited with his son just behind him. As Julia and Alex approached, she could see John's face clearly. He looked directly into her eyes, and there was an outpouring of emotion that moved Julia to the depths of her soul. He did not smile, but seemed to take her in with a loving, if invisible, embrace.

She stood beside him and heard the ceremony as if it were happening to someone else. Not until John took hold of her hand as the couple returned up the aisle did Julia fully enter the present moment. Only then did she fully realize the dramatic change in her own status. There was an intimacy in John's touch that reminded Julia that as of now, her life was changed. A peaceful presence overtook her. Sheer joy was so vibrant it might have been a third person.

A wedding breakfast was served at the Gardiner home. John Jr. started to toast the couple. As the morning wore on, he drank too much champagne and ended the morning in a morose and sullen silence.

Julia changed into a black silk traveling gown. Following the meal, they were taken to the foot of Courtland Street. There the ferry boat, the *Essex*, awaited.

***

John could hardly recognize himself. There had been no happiness in his life to compare to this day. Even with his son's despicable behavior, the presence of this woman at his side, greater than life, buoyed in him an unbelievable joy.

Alexander orchestrated every detail of the day, omitting neither the romantic nor the political aspect of the event.

As they reached the boat, the first group of well-wishers beyond their inner circle greeted them with cheer and good wishes.

John turned to Alex with a questioning look.

Alex was beaming. "I arranged this last night with the local Democrats. No one knows the nature of the occasion, but when they see you and the flowers, they will." John's countenance betrayed his dissatisfaction. Alex continued his explanation, "Mr. President, these are well-wishers. You are the president and a candidate. These people consider themselves your friends. I have kept them at a distance, but to exclude them entirely would place your popularity in peril."

"Popularity? Surely, you jest!"

"You do have friends, sir, just look." A band struck up "Hail to the Chief." Following the musical introduction, the couple was saluted by guns from the *North Carolina* and, ironically, the *Princeton*. There was also a salute from Governor's Island.

John looked at Julia by his side. "What do you say, love?"

She looked up at him, "It's your life, John. I'm only now entering it."

"Are you all right with this? Well, some of it is nonsense."

"I'm fine with it. I shall be fine without it. Our life is one now."

At Jersey City, Julia, the president, and Margaret were taken off the craft. They boarded a train to Washington City, where they were to stop briefly. Then the celebrating couple were to go to Old Point Comfort in Virginia for a brief stay. Margaret and a maidservant went with them as far as Washington City.

Alexander, especially, was pleased at the successful maintenance of secrecy. Later, he wrote to Julia:

> *The city continues full of surprise, and the ladies will not recover in some weeks. At the corners of the streets, in the public places and in every drawing room, it is the engrossing theme. The whole affair is considered one of the most brilliant coups de main ever acted, and I cannot but wonder myself that we succeeded so well in preserving at once the president's dignity and our feelings from all avoidable sacrifice.*[x]

***

The train was chugging, creating a comfortable rhythm. The arrangements in the coach gave Julia time to talk privately with John. "What have your other children said about us, John?"

"Well, I haven't been too exacting in the information I've given." John frowned.

"Do you mean you didn't tell them until it was absolutely necessary, like this morning on the way to church?" Julia interpreted his look. "I must remember that a wrinkled brow is a sign of deception from you." She turned and placed her hand on his forehead.

"It wasn't deception. I just decided that they would absorb the information more discretely if it were not placed in the future tense."

"Let's see. Translated, that means, now they can't try to talk you out if it."

"That's not what I said." John's words were measured. Julia suspected he wanted to be truthful, but not hurt her feelings with the sad news that his children were not thrilled with a step-mother from their own generation.

She turned to face him squarely. "I'm a big girl, John. I can believe that they aren't happy with me. I can win them over in time. Except for John, I don't know about him."

***

The wedding party stopped for the night in Philadelphia. After the arduous trip, the couple finally arrived in their room with real privacy. John saw that Julia was visibly exhausted and he was very tired also. Julia carefully removed her wraps. The maid took their outer clothing for overnight care, and left them. Finally, they were alone for the first time.

John gently put his arms around Julia, who reached up and kissed him expectantly. The results were startling. Suddenly the reality of their new relationship came upon him. With swift and purposeful motion, layers of clothing were removed, and the two found themselves in bed.

John did not know what to expect. Letitia's response had been submissive. He wanted to be gentle and initiate his bride so that she needn't have fear. Yet his restraint was met with an expectant Julia, eager for the experience awaiting her. As he, conscious of her innocence, held back, she became the aggressor. Every sensation delighted her. She showed no reservation.

They were spent. She lay in the crook of his arm, falling asleep. John considered his state, a man married for more than twenty years to one woman, now widowed and again married, this time to a youthful and lusty virgin.

The following day, the entourage resumed their trip to Washington and the White House, now to become Julia's home. By June 27, when they arrived, news of the presidential marriage was very public. At every stop between Philadelphia and Washington, people came to see the happy couple. They were especially curious about Julia, reputed to be beautiful. Now she was to be their First Lady. Excitement was in the air. A dream had descended upon Washington.

Chapter 28

Early Days

The White House calendar took precedence over any suggestion of a honeymoon. Everything began there. Julia had only one day to put the finishing touches on a reception John planned before he left. The staff knew that the Blue Room was to be open to guests upon the president's return. Champagne and light refreshments were ordered for several hundred people. Julia ordered flowers for tables and the piano. Julia and the president, with Margaret, received guests. In the center of the room, a table held a wedding cake and wine.

John Calhoun, now secretary of state, prototype of Southern chivalry, escorted Julia to the bride's table and assisted as she cut and served cake.

"Madame, in the absence of your father—whose absence we all mourn—allow me?" His arm was there, solid, for Julia to lean on.

"You are very kind, sir." She took hold ceremoniously. "But now I do have a president's arm."

"And he is very fortunate to have you as an appendage to his arm!"

Her smile could not have been more alluring as she added, "I hope, sir, to be more than an appendage."

The secretary looked down at the young lady on his arm. Her energy communicated itself. "I'm sure you are."

The reception was a long two hours. John assured Julia, after the last guest departed and the Blue Room was restored, "This won't be the last party."

She was exuberant. "I can hardly wait for the season. This year, my love, we will give the wags a run. It will be wonderful."

She danced around the Blue Room. John first watched her, and then took her in his arms and danced with her. They kissed, and suddenly all thought of the reception was over. Other events were beckoning. The two departed quietly.

Julia wrote to Juliana, *I have commenced my auspicious reign, and am in quiet possession of the Presidential Mansion.*[xi]

***

With Washington still agog over the new First Lady, John and Julia left the city by boat on July 3 to complete the honeymoon. They arrived at Old Point Comfort at one o'clock in the morning for the remainder of their holiday. Colonel Gustavus A. de Russy met them at the landing.

Margaret returned to New York in spite of John's request that she accompany them on the remainder of their wedding trip. He confided to Julia when they were alone, "I'm afraid you'll get bored and lonely when you discover how very demanding my daily work is."

"I'll never be tired of being your wife, and your work will become my work. There is so much to do. Don't worry, my sweet. I'll manage."

John made introductions. "Colonel de Russy, my wife."

The colonel bowed graciously, and extended the welcome that only a Southern gentleman can bestow. He extended his arm. "Ma'am, the hour is late. We should proceed to your quarters at once. The Fort will greet you formally tomorrow." The colonel had a cottage on grounds prepared for them. It was a suite with a well-furnished sitting room and a luxurious bedroom, complete with a canopied bed.

Julia went from room to room. "Oh, John, this is beautiful. Did you order it up?"

"I simply put the colonel in charge. He must have a certain respect for our state in life." The home was reserved for the families of high-ranking officers. Julia started to examine the lace and ribbon, all in white and blue. She turned from the coverlet to John. They were alone again. The time in the White House had been rushed. Now, there would be only the two of them and some leisure. Julia moved purposefully toward John.

The colonel, however, had other ideas concerning their stay at Old Point Comfort. There were parties and social activities. The officers of Fortress Monroe were marched to pay respect to their commander in chief and Julia. She thoroughly enjoyed the ritual. The couple was honored at a dinner aboard a Revenue Cutter. That dinner lasted until three in the morning.

While they were at Fort Monroe, John Jr. arrived. When they found him at home after the dinner, he was waiting in the living room. John showed his surprise. "Son, what brings you here? Did you bring mail from Washington?"

John Jr., again, had too much to drink. He was sullen. Julia was out of the room. "Well, Father, is she good?"

The president squared his shoulders. He had no intention of sharing his most intimate life with his son. "You are being rude."

"She seemed hot, even last year and before, when we played cards. She was playing for high stakes, even then. I guess she won the jackpot this season!"

"Go get some rest, and have a civil tongue in your head when I see you tomorrow." The president strode quickly out of the room.

Alone with Julia, John was somewhat distracted by the unpleasant exchange with his son, but Julia was learning how to attract and keep his attention.

Chapter 29

The Honeymoon Is Over

Upon their return to the White House, Julia at once took charge of their social life. There were afternoon calls. As First Lady, she had every right to expect others to pay the initial call, except, of course, for Dolley Madison. Julia was prepared to visit the Grand Old Lady of Washington. However, Dolley was not about to be pre-empted. She sent her card around in the morning. Precisely at two o'clock, she was ushered into the East Room. Julia entered. "Dolley, it's wonderful to see you!"

The guest's teal satin gown was exactly matched by the feathers in her turban. She brimmed with good cheer, hugging Julia. "My sweet little one! Condolences and congratulations."

"I miss my father, but with John I have a whole new life that he wanted for me. I wish he were here. He'd enjoy it so. But now, it's mine to share with John."

"Cherish every minute of it, sweet. It passes all too quickly."

"John and I look forward to much happiness. But right now, I have work to do. John says our most important goal is to annex Texas, preferably before election. There is so little time."

"Learn to count votes, Julia. You can add to the ayes by entertaining the proper wives. For that matter, you can charm the necessary congressmen. Just listen carefully to their speeches. Know their views, validate what you can, and smile a lot. You will make a difference."

"I must. But come, let's have some tea." Over their china teacups, Julia planned her first dinner with Dolley's help.

"Start small." The grand dame took another pastry and slipped the first bite into her mouth. "Then by the time you have to handle ambassadors and foreign royalty, you will be a pro." She finished the sweet.

Julia pulled a pad of paper from her pocket. "Let's see. I want you there. I need you. And John Jr. must be included."

"Where does the president need influence?"

Julia bit the pencil end. "Well, he worries about Senator Calhoun a lot. We never know what he will say. The problem with Texas is his biggest worry."

"We'll have to get a feeling for how the Texas resolution is breaking in the House of Representatives, and then we will do some homework there. I know a wonderful little gentleman from Tennessee who counts votes. Really counts them. He sits near where I do, and during proceedings I can see him measure how people are responding to the speeches. I think you should meet him."

Julia put her cup aside and leaned over the table. "Who is he? He sounds invaluable."

Dolley looked at the plate of goodies and reached for another. "His name is Andy Johnson. He's an absolute dear, so shy and self-deprecating, but when he speaks he becomes an orator. Sometimes he's short-tempered, but he's really a lamb. Suppose I ask him to bring me next week. You can talk to him."

"That sounds perfect, Dolley. I do appreciate your interest."

I wouldn't have it any other way, my pet." Dolley picked up her napkin and wiped her lips.

***

Another dinner was planned for a week later. Guests gathered in the Blue Room. Dolley arrived early on the arm of a lanky, dark-haired man whom she presented to Julia. "May I present Congressman Andrew Johnson from Tennessee."

Julia held out her hand and offered her warmest smile. "Charmed, Congressman. It's wonderful to see you."

The stranger blushed, turning a deep red. He took Julia's hand and stumbled over, "Likewise."

Suddenly Julia was back at her first dance with a dumbstruck cadet. She laughed softly. "How do you like our Capitol, sir?"

"I . . . well, fine, ma'am."

She was conscious of the rough tweed of his jacket. It was perfectly cut, and gave him an aristocratic air that his halting speech and boyish manner belied.

Dolley spoke, "I've been telling Mrs. Tyler that I think you take uncommon care in analysis of the votes in the

House, Andy. I do hope you will share with her where you have common ground."

Again, he looked at the floor and blushed. "I'd be happy to."

Julia said, "Maybe we could discuss the resolution on Texas at another time?"

"If I can help, I'd be happy to."

Julia drifted from the reception line. She looked over at John, who motioned her to return to his side. "We'll speak again, Congressman, soon."

"You can call me Andy, ma'am."

John and Julia greeted the others. Drinks were served and an air of amiability prevailed. Going into the formal dining room, Secretary Calhoun escorted Julia behind the president and Mrs. Calhoun.

"You must be enjoyin' your new role as First Lady." The secretary's voice was low and intimate.

"Yes, I am. Our time away was wonderful, but the president was eager to return, and I am very glad to be here." They entered the dining room, softly illuminated by candles and the setting sun.

"Ma'am, you are an asset to him in every way."

Julia tipped her head to him in acknowledgment of the compliment. "I plan to be, Mr. Secretary. We anticipate a successful season."

China and crystal sparkled from each place at the table. John sat at the head with Mrs. Calhoun on his right. At his left, Julia was next to the secretary of state. Dolley and

Congressman Johnson were at the foot of the table, and a dozen other guests were between them.

"We're hopin' to add the acquisition of Texas to your accomplishments," Calhoun continued.

"That's John's dearest dream. If I can help in any way . . ."

"Ma'am, just be yourself. That will be more valuable for the president than any other service. You seem to be the perfect hostess."

"I'm learning, Mr. Secretary."

The servants filed in with soup. They filled wine glasses. John proposed a toast. "Here's to the next six months and the miracles we can work in that time."

From near the foot of the table, Justice McLean stood. "Here's to the lady in Washington City that can make miracles happen!" He bowed in Julia's direction. Julia nodded.

Senator Rives stood. "Here's to the team that will overcome the triple adversity of bad press, bad Congress, and bad politics." Nearly everyone laughed.

After the toast, Julia said, "As the press sees it, all politics are bad."

"And nearly all congressmen, ma'am." The justice added, "Maybe both can be touched by grace and charm."

"That is my aim, sir."

Chapter 30
Julia in the White House

John was mildly irritated. He felt he had made his priorities clear. "Robert, these are affairs of state. They come before politics."

"But, Father, if you don't pay attention to politics, you won't have to settle the affairs of state. Someone else will."

John lay down his pen and leaned back in his chair. Robert, visiting from Philadelphia, was making every effort to convince John of the importance of strategy. Robert was stiffly upright. The urgency of his message communicated itself. "Polk isn't well known. People are afraid that Clay will win, but if we support Polk, it will be quite a different matter. Right now, you are splitting the anti-Clay forces. We could be responsible for that bastard winning. But, if you endorse Polk, he'd have a majority, and you will have some hold over the new administration. We can keep our appointees, even obtain some favor."

"I will probably do it in time, Robert, but for now, let's hold on and see what kind of leverage we can gain. We don't know Polk. There is certainly no guarantee he will deal with us. Remember, I'm neither Democrat nor Whig."

***

After John and Julia bade goodbye to Robert, who returned to Philadelphia, they were upstairs in their drawing room. John had a brandy on the table next to him and a newspaper in hand. Julia was playing the guitar. She lay it down and moved nearer to him. "Robert came to talk about politics, didn't he?"

"Yes, he wants me to withdraw my name from candidacy in favor of Polk. But it's my hedge to maintain whatever power I can. Neither party would nominate me. Clay controls the Whigs. Democrats consider me a traitor, even though I am saving their collective neck day by day. So I keep my following, such as it is, separate. Eventually, I suppose I'll have to support Polk, but I'd rather not."

"You've really been nominated officially, haven't you?"

"Well, yes. Our third-party convention is not to be taken too seriously." He chuckled, "Although it was great fun. Supporters do buoy my spirits on the rare occasions when they are all together and saying good things about me." He was thoughtful for a moment. "I think you would enjoy a convention. No women were allowed to vote or speak, but with the bands and hoopla . . . 'Tyler and Texas' was our banner and our motto," his voice rose, "and our song!" Once again the volume increased, "And our platform!"

Julia glowed with appreciation of his theatrics, but soon she turned serious. "What will happen now?"

John spoke slowly and deliberately, "The Democrats named Polk before they even met, but it took them nine ballots to do it. The party that disowned me has named Clay, totally unacceptable."

"If I remember my visits to the galleries of Congress, Polk wasn't the least extraordinary." Her hands were in motion depicting the gallery in the chamber and limiting Polk to a spot on the floor. "He's from the old Jackson crowd. McDuffie says he has zeal worthy of a better cause than Tennessee. He lacks smoothness in oratory, where Clay and Webster set the tone, but Polk does work hard. He never smiles."

John became thoughtful. "I remember Henry Wise was very angry at him once. They started yelling right there on the House floor. I thought it was going to turn into a real fight." John laughed out loud. "Indeed, it was real. Henry tried to induce a duel, but Polk would have no part of it."

Julia continued, "I remember Henry yelling, 'You're a damned little petty tyrant. I mean this personally!'"

"Polk would never bite. He was Speaker, and he knew his powers."

Julia laughed. "Henry Wise will never forgive you if you support him."

"Henry owes us both one. Polk stands well on Texas. At the convention he was a dark horse. Henry had to wear the Van Buren people out, overcome animosity." John took his glass and sipped. "I will stay in the race to insure that my people are treated well after the election. Eventually he will bargain me out of the fray, but not until I've gotten what I want."

"You hate Clay, don't you?" Julia was pensive. "I'm trying to imagine my gentle husband with such passionate anger."

John looked grim. "Clay set out to destroy my administration from the day of Harrison's death. I was first confronted by the Cabinet he controlled. They announced clearly that I should follow a majority vote of their consciences formed by Clay. When I refused this, they resigned en masse, except, of course, for Daniel. Following that, Clay designed a bank bill that he knew I could not support and forced my veto rather than work on compromise lines that I had proposed. He has subverted the Texas issue at every turn."

"Polk will get the credit for Texas, won't he?"

"I suppose so. But that does not worry me one bit. My quiet little resolution, one that raises no furor, is in the hopper. And that piece of work does have friends in the press. It's another reason to defeat Clay. That will be a palpable victory for me."

"What resolution, John?"

"The one that has the United States making an agreement with Texas and passing a resolution affirming it in the House."

"What do you mean?"

"Well, a treaty demands a two-thirds majority from the Senate for approval. There is no issue in God's world that would have two-thirds of the Senate supporting me. But a resolution of the joint Houses needs only a majority approval. And for Texas, I can probably get that. Clay will have to take that blow. His defeat will be a real victory for me, even though it will spell the end of your reign as First Lady."

"My reign as Mrs. John Tyler won't end." She rose, came over to him, placed herself delicately on his lap, and reached for his face, drawing her finger down the side of his cheek.

Chapter 31

Julia's Auspicious Reign

Julia was determined to improve the White House interior. Chairs had not been covered since the Monroe presidency. Paint peeled from the walls. Drapes and curtains were worn and faded.

As fall set in, outside the leaves turned color. Inside the Executive Mansion, men worked well into twilight. The rooms were closed off one by one, while coats of new paint restored the regal nature of the high-ceilinged rooms. She used her personal funds to upholster chairs and sofas. Her taste and good sense prevailed, enhancing each room.

About the chairs, she wrote her mother that they "are all in a state of perfect explosion at every prominent point that presents contacts with the outer garments of the visitors."[xii]

Her concern for taste and fashion went outside as well as in. Julia ordered livery for the coachmen and footmen. They were outfitted with black breeches and coats with velvet bands and sand buckles on their hats. John hesitated when he first saw the new uniforms. "Aren't they a bit . . ." He didn't finish his thought.

"What, John? Regal? I intend they should be. We are the First Family in the nation."

"A plain old black coach has always been good enough for me."

"No! It hasn't. You have settled for a plain old coach. But no more! I am here to remind you that you are president."

John's voice was full of emotion. "And you are my First Lady."

"I am your wife. I'm doing this for posterity, John. We'll be gone, but all of this isn't our personal property. How we live says something to the world. We are a great, beautiful, and rich land. The president's life should reflect that."

Julia wanted her court to be perfect for the coming social season. She intended to use the influence of her person to win support for John's cause. She was at her desk in the family quarters, upstairs. Lists were all around. Her pen was busy. John was reading nearby. She looked up to share her decisions with John. "Margaret will head my court. There are Nannie and Mary Wycliffe, and Mary and Phoebe Gardiner. Oh dear, we must do something about names."

John looked up. "You are a very persuasive woman, dear, but what can you do about given names?"

"Maybe we'll number them: Mary the First and Mary the Second."

"You are imitating royalty again. But who are the Gardiner girls? I thought I knew all of your family."

"They are the daughters of Papa's brother, Saul, and they are just right. They will so love the season. Shelter Island is positively suffocating! You can't imagine what it's like to be stuck in a place like that when you're young and . . ."

"Eager to meet young men?"

Julia smiled at her husband. "Well, yes. Don't you consider that an acceptable activity? Besides, these young men are congressmen, court clerks, and embassy attaches."

"I should not be as contented as I am today if you had not indulged, my dear."

"Phoebe is boy crazy. She loves poetry. She will take every eye in the city. Mary is more quiet and reserved, but I think she will get along well. Actually, she's engaged to a student who is in Germany. She can enjoy without committing herself. Alice will be a fine member of my court, too. She's old enough now. Priscilla, Mary, and Elizabeth have had enough of Washington for the present, don't you think, dear?" Julia returned to her list. "Of course, we could ask them."

"No, that won't be necessary. Alice can represent our family just fine." If John was unhappy about Julia's decision to exclude his older girls, he gave no indication. "I do appreciate the way you are endearing Alice. It's important to me that you two get along. There is life after Washington."

"I know, but right now life in Washington is my main worry! Oh, I do want David here through the season. Alex is busy with your political future. He won't settle here long enough to help. Both my brothers would be perfect escorts for the court."

"Be careful about calling them the 'court.' Remember that you are not in Europe now, and Americans can be very touchy about royalty."

"John, my love, I should not do anything to hurt you." She left her desk and was on his lap before the words were out of her mouth. She kissed him eagerly, jumped up, and returned to her desk. "I'm so glad Dolley is near. She is such a help to me. She lets me know when everything is all right, and tells me when I need to fix something. Margaret will be with us, so I must find another unattached man. Why don't you bring Caleb home?"

John looked up from his papers. "Wasn't he a suitor of yours?"

"Of course, everyone was at one time or another," Julia's face softened into a smile, "until you. Then they didn't matter anymore."

"Mmm, if I do bring him home, be sure he sits next to Margaret or Dolley. I need you to work on reluctant members of Congress, or maybe you could tame Secretary Calhoun."

Julia came over behind him and gently turned his head to her. "I've already started the process, my dear."

Her guest lists were growing, as was her ability to manage larger parties. At one dinner, the largest event so far, she placed herself between Attorney General John Nelson and Secretary of State Calhoun. Later, she gave the secretary rave reviews. "He whispered poetry in my ear, and generally treated me to the best of the chivalrous Old South."

John's reply was good-natured. "Well, I must look out for a new secretary of state if Calhoun is to stop writing dispatches and go to repeating verses. Remember you have a duty to perform with him."

Julia's eyes twinkled. "Oh, John, you know I do love older men."

Julia wrote to her mother concerning the plans for the coming social season. *I intend to do something in the way of entertaining that shall be the admiration and talk of the Washington world. I plan weekly levees and formal receptions for every possible reason and several grand functions. My reign may be brief, but it will be memorable.*

***

At the last possible moment, John formally withdrew from the presidential race and threw his support to Polk. Robert had attempted negotiation with the candidate to assure that John's appointments were safe. He received only vague generalities rather than firm promises, but there was enough good will offered to make John's support for Polk possible.

In November, Polk took the vote by a razor-thin majority. He received 1,337,000 popular votes to Clay's 1,229,000. In the Electoral College, that translated to 170 votes to 105 for Clay. John analyzed the published numbers. "I feel my withdrawal made Polk's victory possible. His margin was 5,000 in New York. Nearly half of that was from New York City. Alex's work easily accounted for the number. Robert, in Philadelphia, carried Pennsylvania. Virginia went for Polk. Alex assures me that my withdrawal was pivotal in each of these cases. If that's so, our newly-elected president can thank me for not pursuing my third-party plans."

"Keep those forces intact, John. They may come in handy again someday."

"My dear Julia, doesn't your pretty head ever rest?"

"You are a great man. And no one knows what the future may bring. I just think that when you've created something good, you should preserve it for future use. Even if not for you, it might influence another election. A third-party could do very surprising things. The country must remember you. We will see to that."

***

Margaret's return to Washington was a matter of great moment. She arrived in the early afternoon. She and Julia were talking breathlessly in the upstairs hall. John came up the stairs. "I heard the clamor. It can only be that the pearl of the White House has returned." He hugged Margaret.

She reached up and kissed him on the cheek. "To my favorite brother-in-law."

"Given the number of your sisters, you don't have many more, I hope. Oh, Margaret, I am glad to see you. I think Julia needs your company."

The cousins arrived. The Wycliffe girls lived in Washington, so were frequent visitors upstairs, especially during the day. Gales of laughter could be heard all over the mansion. When Alice came home, she completed the ensemble.

The girls devised a game entirely too loud and too childish for White House protocol, especially when the First Lady was playing. One of the girls would grab a poker from a fireplace. She was "it." She was to invent a pun on an eligible bachelor's name. When she did, the girl nearest her would win the poker, and the process would start over. The girls could be heard running short distances. Margaret took the poker in her hands and chased Phoebe, crying, "Phoebe has the greatest Polk." She touched Phoebe with her free hand and passed the poker.

"But Nannie sits on a Cushing all day long." Phoebe handed the poker to Nannie.

"In the end, Mary got Wise." Nannie handed her the poker and ran to the family parlor, dropping exhausted onto the sofa.

"Ugh, he's a shriveled-up, old prune." Mary and Phoebe followed her. The gales of laughter echoed through the mansion. The others, including Julia, trailed in. Although the running slowed, puns did not.

"Alice will lean on McLean." The girls all turned to the president's daughter. She took the poker, laughing.

"No, I want to Fillmore of my dance card." She handed the poker to Margaret.

"Do I get my Pickens?" She was a master of the game.

Phoebe, sitting on the settee, leaned forward to share a confidence. "Would you believe? After I met Fayette McMullen and talked to him just the shortest time, he proposed to me! 'I'm enchanted by your vivaciousness, ma'am,' he said. But he's not nearly as wonderful as Stephen Douglas. That frontier charm will beat Virginia's polish any day."

Her sister, Mary, said, "Senator Douglas is awfully short. Of course he is interesting. He can make civics as wonderful as literature."

Phoebe and Margaret, in unison, said, "Well there is always Major Polk."

Alice asked, "Who is he?"

Julia answered, "He's the brother of the new president. Handsome, charming, and," her voice dropped, "from Tennessee."

***

When Juliana arrived, she was critical of such events within the White House. She talked to Julia privately. "You should be more proper. You are not a child, and you hold an office of great significance."

"John calls me his child bride."

"But, I can assure you, he doesn't want you acting like a child in front of visitors."

"Oh, Mother. I know how to act on state occasions, and when nothing is happening officially, it's good for everyone to have some fun."

"John's position is most important. His popularity is precarious. You could compromise his standing if the press were to detect this foolishness."

"Mother, John's greatness doesn't depend on solemn quietude. He'll be remembered for his ascendency to president, his plans for Texas, and relations with England. And even if he isn't, he's done all those things. That's what's important."

"Impressions are important, Julia. Do not lose sight of that."

Chapter 32
The Thomas Incident

Society hailed the coming season as the most brilliant Washington has ever beheld. Polk's victory was seen as a White House victory, and John had Julia beside him. For the first time in many years, life looked positively joyous. John's feelings about Clay were public knowledge, and Polk's position on Texas was clearly a victory for Tyler.

Following the election was Christmas preparations. "This year will be like no other. The girls and I will decorate to a fare-thee-well." Julia provided evergreen garlands to be in all the parlors and candles from New York City. The ladies-in-waiting spent afternoons winding the green and adding red and white ribbon until the room looked like Christmas presents turned inside out.

Margaret was in charge of decorating the dining room. Julia entered just as Margaret was placing the last touches on her work. "We look like a pine forest."

"Well, I've added ribbons and candles to relieve the monotony. But if you want originality, I could do something outlandish; decorate in Halloween colors, plant tropical flowers all over the rooms."

"No, the conventional Christmas colors and wreaths will do very well." She surveyed the handiwork. "We look like a fairyland."

***

Sitting at his desk late one evening, John reviewed the changes in his life: Letitia was a good wife. She was ill when he came to the White House. As a result, she never participated in this phase. Elizabeth and Priscilla made lovely hostesses, but it was a sacrifice on their parts. They served out of necessity, not with the sheer exuberance of youth that his Julia was daily demonstrating. Looking back, he realized that Julia's attitudes and lifestyle were immersing him in a totally new way of living. His had been a sober point of view, made more so by Letitia's stern and sparse ways. He remembered when he and Letitia, together, had condemned the waltz as vulgar. *Men and women do not position themselves that intimately in public.* Now not only the waltz, but all the new dances could be heard here. He and Julia were planning to introduce the polka at the New Year's Eve party. He was buoyant, energized by her innocent approach to life. Even the dramatic political defeats he suffered were mitigated by her charm, her life, her confidence in him and in herself.

The White House, too, was showing the difference. Laughter could be heard these days. The girls ran about making plans, as if the social season were a massive birthday party. Julia darted in and out of the presidential study, interrupting John on a whim, hugging him, kissing him passionately, and leaving again just as suddenly. John always had a smile on his lips; something new for him, for he had been a solemn and sensible lad and had grown into a serious young man. Julia made all of life better!

Christmas Eve was celebrated with a large dinner party. There was merriment in the Blue Room, where the mansion's main Christmas tree was aglow. After the guests were gone and the house guests retired, Julia went upstairs. "I'll be along in a minute, love." John turned down the hall. He was surprised at his own delight in playing Santa Claus. He returned to his office, where Julia's gift was hidden. His heart was beating rapidly as he raced up the stairs. He opened the bedroom door. "My dear, I have a special gift that I want you to see while we are alone."

Julia turned to find John carrying a large, gold bird cage, covered.

"What . . .?" He watched her eyes grow big. She took the cage from him. Even as she looked around for a place to set it, her face broke into a delightful grin. She placed the cage on the table and removed the fitted cover to reveal a tiny, pale yellow canary. "Oh, John, how wonderful! I shall love him forever." She looked at the diminutive bird a long time. Then she turned to John, put her arms around him, and said, "I think we shall call him Johnny Ty. He will be part of our family as long as we live. Merry Christmas, John."

John put his arms around his bride and thanked God for the gift of life.

***

When Julia's portrait arrived, completed by E. G. Thompson of New York, she did not like it.

"I look like a dainty, little old lady."

John chuckled. "I think you look quite lovely in that portrait, my dear."

"It's not one whit like me. I don't like it, and that should settle the matter. I will have it redone."

"Talk to Margaret and your mother before you do anything radical. It is really very lovely."

Within a week, B. O. Tyler of New York was commissioned to provide a more fashionable version of Julia for posterity. The portrait was only one of Julia's public relations moves.[xiii]

***

"John, have you noticed a Mr. Thomas? He's been at every open house we've had here. I believe he's a *Herald* correspondent." John was studying the minutes of a Cabinet meeting, while Julia embroidered. Julia glanced up and observed that John was not paying attention. "I think I shall approach him to become my secretary." She made the statement like a cat pouncing upon its prey.

John's reaction was casual. "Nonsense, my love. You enjoy doing your own correspondence."

She dropped her work and went to John, throwing her arms around him from the back of his chair. "You don't understand. He won't be doing my correspondence."

John dropped his papers and reached behind to catch her. "What will he be doing, this secretary?"

He tickled. She giggled. "He will assure us of space in the newspaper that is favorable on the society page." John frowned. She rubbed his brow. "I'll pay for it out of my allowance, silly. I know your official budget doesn't allow for such extras."

"Whatever pleases you, my sweet, but I don't want this secretary meddling politically," he said as he kissed her.

Thomas was installed as Julia's press secretary over John's mild objections. A newspaper article from New York referred to Julia as the "presedentrix." Mr. Thomas brought her the clipping. Julia's face broke into a broad grin. She ran to John's office. "Look at this!" She handed John the newspaper. Overall, the story wasn't flattering. It implied that John was weak and now there was another, possibly evil, influence on him.

"Did you read it all, Julia?"

She took back the article and scanned it. "Oh, John, that's not it at all. I simply loved the title! But . . ."

"Maybe your new press secretary can establish the title without the uninvited connotations." John patted her and returned to his work.

She returned to the room where Thomas was at work. "Mr. Thomas, I want you to establish this title not in a bad way, but in a good one. Do you understand?"

"You would like to be a presidentrix without the title detracting from Mr. Tyler's stature. Is that it?"

"Exactly. Can you manage that?"

He bowed ceremoniously. "Of course, madam." Within a very short time, the title was simply how people thought about the couple in the White House: the president and his presidentrix.

One day, Julia overheard Mr. Thomas very casually asking John, "Was that Mr. Calhoun I saw leaving?"

John's answer was guarded. "That is not social news. He is the secretary of state."

Julia motioned. "Mr. Thomas, please step into the parlor." She was growing suspicious of his ingratiating manner. "Here's the guest list for Saturday's levee. Please do not bother the president. He obtains sufficient coverage from the press."

Thomas had his hat in hand. "I'm just tryin' to be helpful, ma'am."

"Or are you trying to obtain a scoop?" Julia noted a scowl on his face as she dismissed him. A few weeks later, the *Herald* printed an anonymous story that Julia was pregnant. "That does it! I will fire him tomorrow!" She was furious. "Not only is it not true, it would hurt you to publish it, even if it were."

John appeared somewhat calmer about the event. "It could be so, my darling."

"But it's not, and it won't be until we can enjoy such an event."

"You are a strong-willed young lady. I don't know how you can control such events, when—" Discretion stopped John from completing the thought.

Mr. Thomas was summarily dismissed. Not only was Julia not pregnant, but at the time, such an event would have, indeed, added to John's difficulty.

***

Julia started the project as a dinner for the elite of Washington's social life. "John," she asked, "how many people are the crème de la crème of the diplomatic corps?"

John was working on state papers at his desk in the family quarters. It was an unusually quiet night. The visitors were at a play. Only he and Julia were at home. By now he was used to the noise and laughter caused by Julia's "court." Julia wanted his undivided attention, and he preferred hers to the affairs of state. He put the work aside and moved over to his easy chair.

"Ambassadors? Oh, thirty—with their wives?"

"Of course with their wives, Mr. President. You and I are going to give a farewell party. I'd like it to be elite and elegant, something to remember forever."

"That is how you've been entertaining ever since you took office."

"I think we should have it in February. That allows a month. If we wait too late, everyone will start leaving Washington, and I won't have the proper guests. If we have it too early, it won't be a farewell. Let's see." Her expression changed. "Oh, not then, it would be the anniversary of Papa's . . ."

He drew her close. "No, we will not plan it on the twenty-eighth of February." She could feel the warmth and security of his arms enfolding her. "But there are twenty-seven other days in the month. Certainly one of them would be right. Who, besides the ambassadors, will come?"

"Well, we'll have the Cabinet, of course. I'm so glad they're our friends. It must have been awful when you had those other men."

"Yes, well, we weren't entertaining much then."

"Oh, John, that was before . . ."

"Before Letitia died? Yes. It was. But I was a different man then."

She put her arms around him and drew closer. "I can hardly remember a time when we weren't man and wife." They remained quiet, each pondering the changes in life.

John broke the silence. "So far we have the Cabinet and the diplomatic corps. Who else?"

"Well, our friends in Congress and their wives. And I think I will send some select invitations to New York and Virginia."

"Your family and mine?"

Julia laughed quietly. "Do you think Letty will come?"

"Maybe, if Alice asks her to. But I'm certain Elizabeth and William will. She wants to see your court. And Priscilla and Robert would. Would you consider inviting Mr. and Mrs. Ritchie? He's the editor of the Virginia newspaper out of Richmond."

"Of course, my love."

"And shall we invite the president-elect and his wife?" John seemed hesitant.

Julia considered the question carefully. "I think not. We will take care of Sahara Sarah and her president later on. If

Dolley's description is even half right, she would put a damper on the party all by herself."

"You give her a lot of credit to put a damper on one of your occasions!"

"Oh, it's more than that. This is our night. Their time will come." She jumped from his lap, ran to the desk, and started making lists.

***

"Margaret, you contact the printer. Here are the guests' names. It started small, but it isn't any more."

Margaret took the many papers, sat down, and started sorting. She found the appropriate paper and remade the list carefully. The Cabinet became Mr. and Mrs. John Calhoun and Mr. and Mrs. Thomas Ewing. After a long period of diligence, she looked up. "Julia, do you know how many people you have here?"

"A lot. How many?"

"I have a thousand invitations. That's two thousand people. And I'm still untangling your lists."

"Well, it certainly won't be as elite as I'd hoped. But we will make up for that by having it as grand as can be." She left her notes and twirled around the parlor. "The waltz and polka, and it will all be at my command. Nothing will begin until I say so, and everything will end when I say."

Margaret put her pen down. "You can tell this party when to start, but you won't be able to tell it when to end. Parties have a way."

"Nonsense! When the president yawns and says it's over, that's the end."

"He can annex Texas before he can stop one of your parties."

"He'll have a party of his own." Julia's quip was lost on Margaret.

***

Meanwhile, servants cleaned. The wine cellar was enlarged. There would be champagne in abundance, as well as hams from Virginia, local seafood, apples from New York state, even barbecue from the frontier. "Every good thing to eat from all over the land." Julia was in high spirits as the plans developed.

Juliana set a departure date prior to the February eighth event. "Oh, Mother, you must be here. I need you."

"I don't see that you do. I am a widow in mourning, you know. And this isn't to my taste."

"Oh, Mama, please stay. If you go away, who will put us in order and worry properly? You always say I'm a flit, and the girls are twits, and no one keeps tabs on details like you do!"

Juliana considered her child, thought for a moment, and decided. "I could still be home by the middle of the month. Maybe—"

"Good. Now will you write Alex and tell him he must change his plans and come, and Uncle Saul Gardiner? It will be his last chance to see Mary and Phoebe at court . . . and David."

"Julia, we could just publish an invitation in the *Daily News!*"

***

The spacious rooms had been redecorated. The small platform where John and Julia sat with her court surrounding them was in the Blue Room with dancing in the East Room. The Marine Band in scarlet uniform was commissioned to play. The girls wore white. Julia's dress had a fine black net over the waist and hips. She had pearls laced into her luxurious dark hair. John was tall and elegant. They received guests until the waltz started.

"Now, my dear," Julia stood, "I'm opening with Secretary Wilkins. We can dance later. You work on the wives of reluctant congressmen." Julia was whispering to John, who developed a sly smile at his wife's analysis.

It was nearly three in the morning when the last guest bid the couple goodnight. House guests, one by one, retired. John and Julia went upstairs. Halfway up, John turned and looked down over that expanse of the downstairs. It was the sad disarray that is the aftermath of successful entertainment.

"We've said it before, and we are proving it! They're wrong! I am not without a party."

Chapter 33

The Departure

Dolley arranged for Julia to meet Sarah Polk early in March.

Julia and Dolley were seated in the Madison Library with ubiquitous French pasties and the samovar, awaiting the newcomer.

"What's she like?" Julia was in a soft, plaid, two-piece gown. Her dark green hat matched the green in the plaid, and the petite yellow feather echoed the yellow in her suit. A frilly ascot softened her image.

Dolley was thoughtful. "She's different."

"Different from what?"

"You and me."

Julia laughed. "Are you and I the same?"

"Well, we see a lot of things the same. You're kind and happy. You like to have a good time."

"Doesn't everyone?"

Dolley rose. Her bright purple taffeta gown swished through the room as she framed the answer. She turned from the window to face Julia. "Not everyone does. Some people enjoy being dour and grim."

"Don't tell me Sarah is one of those . . ."

"I fear she is." They heard the bell and waited for the serving girl to come to the door. Dolley started to go into the hall, but Mrs. Polk was at the door. Dolley greeted her, "My dear Sarah, we've been waiting for you. Do come in. May I present Julia Tyler?"

Julia saw a tall, angular woman all in black. Her dress was severe, with neither bustle nor crinoline. Her hat, while fashionable, was understated and square, giving the impression of a period at the end of a declarative sentence. Julia rose and held out her hand. It was barely touched by Sarah's gloved one.

"Charmed." Sarah's voice had a flat, nasal quality.

"I'm pleased to have an opportunity to meet you, Mrs. Polk, before we share the formalities of exchange."

"I shall be attending as few of these such affairs as possible. I leave that to others."

"We are planning some evenings where the men can gather to exchange views informally. I hope you will join us. It will be pleasant—"

"The men's views are well-known. I do not believe that pleasure and business mix well."

"I hope that your term as First Lady softens that view."

Dolley had been a silent spectator. She stood just behind Mrs. Polk. As her eye briefly caught Julia's, Dolley looked up to heaven prayerfully.

***

As the season's end came upon the Tylers, there was packing, and there were goodbyes. John and Julia began gathering their personal materials from their desks. Julia remained buoyant through the efforts, but one evening she came upon John looking out a window onto the grounds, still bleak with winter protection and without the promise of new life that would soon show. She put her arms around his waist and leaned her head against his chest. "What is it?"

"I'm just thinking about what has been, and . . . how little we could do."

She reached up and turned his head to see her face. "Just think what you have done! Future generations will know that you secured Texas. You established ascendency upon the death of a president. You firmly drew the border of Northern United States, and you held our land together when others wanted to tear it apart."

"It sounds as if you want to make a success of my failure."

"It is not failure, John. It only seems that way through the press. Your success is very real."

He looked down at her. "My greatest success is winning your love. Just look at our last week." Julia drew nearer, and together they gazed at the early stars. "It was a good time, my love, to the very end."

"Polk and Sarah will take over."

"Yes, and how different it will be."

***

On the following Sunday, the president-elect and his wife visited the White House formally. John and Julia received them in the East Room. Mrs. Polk was in black velvet which, though understated, was a Paris original. Her back was rigid. Julia observed and thought how graceful a touch of lace would be around her collar. She greeted the couple and suggested that President Polk and John could adjourn to his office, while she and Mrs. Polk examined the upstairs. Julia dipped her head and slightly bent her knees, suggesting a curtsy. She felt Mrs. Polk standing stiffly alongside.

Both men nodded in agreement. John kissed Julia gently.

"Come with me, Mrs. Polk, to see your home for the future."

"This will never be home to me. It's too . . . well, too public."

"You may get used to it. Life goes on. Your family is about. Affairs of state are ever-present, but it can be home, too."

"I think it is better that it remain the Executive Mansion, a very public place. It is so easy to influence foreigners' vision of us."

Julia appeared thoughtful. "I believe hospitality benefits the public image, especially from this vantage point. And certainly an image of vitality helps." She could feel the visitor's disdain.

***

In the evening, John and Julia went to Fuller's Hotel. Departure to Richmond was to be by boat in the early morning.

More well-wishers joined them. Dinner was graced with speeches, mostly eulogies that said the good things so scarcely proclaimed in the Tyler administration.

It was 8:10 a.m., a blustery, winter-like morning. The sun peered over a dark cloud-cluster as John and Julia left the hotel to walk to the dock. They were detained in the lobby for a few minutes. Well-wishers wanted to say goodbye. When they came along the dock expecting to board ship, they saw it had already weighed anchor and was moving out to the channel. John waved frantically at the sailor, who waved back. Fortunately, the couple could not hear what occurred on the boat.

"Sir, you left the president waiting on the dock!" A mate approached the captain at the wheel.

"Hell, Polk's in the White House."

On the dock, the forlorn couple stood watching. John sighed. "It's not the end of the world."

Julia, beside him, was thoughtful. *How I take this last indignity will influence him, maybe for the rest of his life.* "Indeed, it is not, my dear. I think you have more well-wishers who did not have an opportunity to speak to you. Our delayed departure is just as well."

They returned to their room at the hotel. Julia was solemn, but her chin was high. "I wanted to be away from here, since we decided not to attend the Polk's ball."

"Pretend we are away from here, love. Sarah's ball is no place for you. You are meant to have such ceremonies, not attend others'."

***

At nine p.m., with no farewells and no admiring crowd, the ex-president and his beautiful, regal wife boarded the boat quite unattended. As they departed down the Potomac, Julia looked back at the city she loved. "John, look, something is burning!"

Flames and smoke were billowing toward the moonlit sky. It was later that they discovered the National Theater burned to the ground, taking several adjoining buildings with it. John turned, put his arms around his wife, and watched the flames and smoke.

"Well, Julia, that is no longer a concern of ours. We have another community to care for."

"I wonder what's burning." Julia's voice was strained.

"Our past."

"No, never. We must tell our story!"

"It sounds as if you want to make a success of my failure."

"There is no failure, John. History will validate you."

"With your love, I know only success. We are on our way home." John concluded, "And I'll never again be a man without a party!"

Obituaries

The Honorable John Tyler, eighteenth president of the United States, was laid to rest in Hollywood Cemetery on January 18, 1862.

He is survived by his second wife, Julia Gardiner Tyler, who resides in the family home outside Richmond, Sherwood Forest, near Williamsberg. Tyler served in the Legislature of the Confederate States.

Tyler lay in state within the confines of the Confederate Congress. His casket was covered with the Confederate flag and a wreath of roses and evergreens.

Several thousand loyal followers visited his remains. Congress [Confederate] devoted the day to eulogizing the one-time president of the United States.

Services were at the Episcopal Church of St. Paul. Jefferson Davis headed the dignitaries attending. The assembly following his remains to the cemetery consisted of more than 150 vehicles.

He is buried on a knoll overlooking the James River.

Henry Wise characterized the man in his eulogy. John "was an honest, affectionate, benevolent, loving man who had fought the battle of his life bravely and truly, doing his whole great duty without fear, though not without much unjust reproach."[xiv]

Tyler ended the second Seminole War, cut the US Army by 33 percent, quelled Dorr's rebellion in 1841, avoided war with Great Britain in 1841 (conflict involved Maine and New Brunswick), *agreed to a ban on slave trade, annexed Texas by a slight of hand trick, and ended the Monroe Doctrine.*

Julia Gardiner Tyler, aged seventy, died July 10, 1889, in Richmond, Virginia. She was buried next to her husband and attended by four of their surviving children, Lonnie, Guardie, Pearl, and their youngest, Fitz.

Father Charles A. Donahoe celebrated a well-attended Requiem Mass.

Somewhat to the surprise of her Southern followers, Mrs. Tyler died a Roman Catholic. Bishop-elect Augustine Van de Vyvr of Richmond officiated at her funeral. He paid her the following tribute: "Her private life was as conspicuous for the practice of virtues as her public life was admirable for the distinguished ability with which she discharged the duties of her exalted position."

Mrs. Tyler was born and raised in New York. After she married President Tyler, her sympathies became clearly Southern. Although she moved to New York during the Civil War for the safety of her children, she continued to be critical of new policies, especially the abolition of slavery. She was quite outspoken about her feelings, accusing the gentry of the North of treating factory workers with less humanity than the South allowed slaves.

In spite of ideological differences, Congress allowed Mrs. Tyler a pension based on the service of her husband as president of the United States.

Endnotes

i   Seager, Robert. *And Tyler Too: A Biography of John and Julia Gardiner Tyler* (p. 36).

New York: McGraw-Hill, 1963.

ii   Seager, Robert (p. 13).

iii   Seager, Robert (p. 135–140).

iv   Seager, Robert (p. 159).

v   Seager, Robert (p. 178).

vi   Seager, Robert (p. 15).

vii   Seager, Robert (p. 198).

viii   Seager, Robert (p. 2).

ix   Seager, Robert (p. 3).

x   Seager, Robert (p. 2).

xi   Seager, Robert (p. 9).

xii   Seager, Robert (p. 594).

xiii   Seager, Robert (p. 472).

About the Author

*"Terri is a political activist. She served as committeeman
and delegate to the State Democratic Committee, attended
two national conventions, and served her local community
as trustee."*
—John LaFalce, Member of US Congress for
eighteen years over the terms of four presidents

Terri Mudd, a frequent contributor to the "My View"
column of *The Buffalo News*, is a longtime resident of Lewiston,
New York, a village on the Niagara River near Lake Ontario.
She has been active in politics most of her adult life, attending
two national conventions and being elected to serve her
community on the local Village Board. An abiding human
interest in matters great and small has informed her writing,
and she is a keen observer of how people engage in conversation. Using dialogue to advance the lively tale she
tells in this, her first novel, she relates the political traits
and unconventional courtship of two largely forgotten but
important historical figures in the era before the Civil War.
Aside from her own literary endeavors, she continues to
facilitate her long-running seminar at the Niagara Falls
Public Library.